MW00945558

The Known Stranger

Volume 1—Inner-city Beat
A Novel and Mystery

Rachelle Hollie Guillory

To: Jacqueline

Enjoy! God

Blessings

Rachelle

TTBOD

You're the most pleasant soror!

Writers Club
San Jose   New York   Lincoln   Shanghai

Chicago 2000

The Known Stranger

All Rights Reserved © 2000 by Rachelle Hollie Guillory

No part of this book may be reproduced or transmitted in any form or by any means, graphic, electronic, or mechanical, including photocopying, recording, taping, or by any information storage or retrieval system, without the permission in writing from the publisher.

Published by Writers Club Press
an imprint of iUniverse.com, Inc.

For information address:
iUniverse.com, Inc.
620 North 48th Street
Suite 201
Lincoln, NE 68504-3467
www.iuniverse.com

ISBN: 0-595-09459-7

Printed in the United States of America

Volume I of IV

For my mother, *Dr. Katie Lee Brown*,
my daughter, *Jazmyn Monét Childress*
and my son, *Dale Robert Childress II.*
Three souls who will fondly and lovingly
occupy an infinite abode in my heart!
An eternity of love,
W-W

Epigraph

The consequence of loving is multifarious
Some victories, some defeats
Our quest for love and passion,
The act of mere coquetry
Misconstrued with attraction
Affinity erroneously perceived as love
Forever lost, our innocence
Heightened by suspect
Oft times discovering we did not know
Those we believe we loved
Who we cast our hopes
Our dreams
Our hearts
Our lives
Strangers though known!

© 1999—Rachelle Guillory

Foreword

I was hooked on *The Known Stranger* from beginning to end. Never have I picked up a book that kept my attention to the point where I could not put it down. Rachelle Guillory keeps the reader's attention with her humor, easy-reading writing style and intriguing story line. This book is an extremely interesting novel that I recommend all readers to make a part of their book collection. On the day I read *The Known Stranger*, my company had arrived for a dinner party I was giving. I could not entertain my guests until I finished this book. For me, that is unheard of. *The Known Stranger* is definitely a keeper!

Margaret Evans,
High School Vice Principal

Preface

The pleasure I received as I wrote this book is why it came into existence. As I place pen to paper, or actually fingertips to keyboard, the story line of my books quickly and easily unfolds. This book by no means was written with the intention to belittle or degrade the image of the African American male or any man for that matter. The exposé written within the walls of this book are fictitious accounts of a man who loved a bit too much, made several mistakes and paid for them. Errs one of the main characters in this book made are unfortunately not unheard of in our society. If we search within our hearts and find a key to unlock the inner most part of the hearts of the ones we love, we may find a stranger within. This book is a gift and testament to the many women who woke up one day and found a stranger that lay beside them. You are not alone. Of course, life gives us signals by which to recognize the true strangers within our lives. Let us not fail to listen to the warning signs of our built-in discernment antennas.

Acknowledgments

Without support there is no foundation. Without another ear, who will hear? Without another hand, assistance is nonexistent. Without another shoulder, who can one lean? Without sisters and brothers, there is no support. Without another, there is no sister or brother. Without you, I would not be! Therefore, to each of the following sisters and brothers, who have proven to be the support system on which I have learned I can depend, I sincerely extend my thanks to you:

First I honor and thank God, who has bestowed upon me myriad talents that I will utilize as long as He continues to use this vessel in which my soul resides. For truly without Him, I would be NOTHING.

My family for their love and encouragement—Including, but of course not limited to:

Dr. Katie Lee Brown *(my ever-dependable supporter)*, Jazmyn Childress, Dale Childress II, Paulette Wills, Rosalind and Leyton Morgan, Carol and Craig Carpentar, George and Annabelle Jackson, Dorothy and Charles Thompson, Mozella Marks, Bruce Wills and Aralee Baptiste, Otis Wills, Delma Guillory-Loeb, Leann Guillory, Wesley and Alice Guillory. To my sister Rosalind, I thank you for your love and **every** aspect of your support! And, my sister Carol, I thank you for your love and gentle spirit! To Elizabeth Guillory, my soror and cousin, thank you!

My friends, *personal and business* (truly not in order of importance):

Mrs. Hildreth Lewis, for your ever-listening ear and gentle spirit, I thank you.

Four of my longest and dearest friends: Theresa Cummings-Schorzman, Beverly Foley, Deborah and Alice Nicholas. I thank you four for your undying friendship, tolerance and support!

Margaret Evans, thank you for your assistance in editing and proofing *The Known Stranger* for me. I needed the extra set of eyes! You exhibit the essence of sisterhood!

Staci Shands, Publicist supreme! Thanks for your expert advice and your much-appreciated professional criticism of my work! Don't forget I still need your help.

Cassandra Collins-Davis, what can I say? You have demonstrated the spirit of friendship. Thanks for having my back!

Margaret Evans, Joy Higgins, Staci Shands, and Dona Ventura: for reading and critiquing *The Known Stranger* before its publication. Your comments were appreciated.

The Incredible women of Inglewood Alumnae Chapter, Delta Sigma Theta Sorority, Incorporated: I thank you for our Dependable, Substantial and Tenacious sisterhood.

Stacey J. Brown, Beverly Dummett, Todd Rodgers, Dr. Thelma James Day, Paula Ruttone and Eun Mee Ju: Your positive remarks regarding my work encouraged me and kept me climbing the ladder!

Mrs. Vera Chappelle, thank you for your encouragement and example to follow!

I extend special thanks to ALL of the individuals who bought my first book of poetry, *Expressions of Soul*, which I self-published. Your belief in my poetic skills and my writing ability encouraged me to continue this journey! It is my prayer that you will love this work and that we will continue this journey together.

iUniverse.com and Barnes and Noble: I appreciate the opportunity you have provided to writers like me! This effort has encouraged and inspired me.

Introduction

The Known Stranger, first of a four book series befittingly titled *Inner-city Beat*, is an account of the mysterious cases two African American detectives are challenged to solve. Detectives Dale Jackson and Randall Viccers are senior and junior detectives on the force, respectively. Detective Randall Viccers, the youngest of the pair, believes he renders order to Detective Jackson's much otherwise chaotic, yet seasoned method of handling the job at hand. Detective Jackson asserts that his partner Randall Viccers pays too much attention to detail and that his theory of logic distorts his view of the answer to the mysteries.

Although their personalities often clash, this duet wittingly and professionally solve the murder cases they're presented with—proving that opposites do attract. As the answer to each of their cases unfolds, the reader will be spellbound, making it difficult to close the book without knowing the solution to the mystery of "who done it". The *Inner-city Beat* series will become a part of your reading collection after you have read this first book in the series.

One

The phone rang at about 3:36 a.m. He knew it was the department. "Somebody's killing somebody again," Detective Dale Jackson whispered to himself. It's sad to think that homicides are a normal routine for people like him, but they are. Anyway, he was certain that there would be nothing different or abnormal about this case than any of his other cases. He was also sure of one other thing, work would start early for him that morning.

"It betta' be important," was his answer as he picked up the receiver, purposely eluding any amenities. It was the Captain. His voice was fresh, as if he had been awake for hours. Captain Capria informed Detective Jackson that there had been a bombing on the seventeenth floor in one of the twin tower buildings in Century City. He wasn't sure if any people were on the floor at the time. From the surface it looked as if only that particular floor was targeted. The Captain instructed Jackson to call Viccers, his partner. "The two of you need to go down there immediately and check it out," he said. "Okay, Cap," was Jackson's reply. "I'll get Viccers and we'll go down there right away."

The Captain was a short, heavy, slightly graying Italian with a heavy New York accent. He is also known as a professional chain smoker. When he talks, he simultaneously coughs and picks his nose. The entire 37th precinct of the Los Angeles Police Department agreed one day that talking to him was like listening to someone attempting to start a car. Except, Cap's finger is the key, his nose is the ignition and his throat is the engine. You know the scenario. You keep trying and trying to start your car but it just doesn't quite turn like it should. Well, the Captain would rev and rev that engine in his throat, but it never turned over. Everyone in the department tried to clear the Captain's throat for him. Jackson once said, "it's like listening to a speaker who had the world's most stubborn frog in his throat. You know what I mean. You try to make him get the hint to clear his throat by coughing suddenly, or loudly clearing your own throat. AHEM!! AHEM!! But he never catches the hint. So, all through his speech you're coughing and clearing your throat and coughing and clearing your throat—because now you really feel as if there's a huge wad of phlegm stuck in the back of yours."

It's not clear why many of the officers called the captain "Cap." It could be that he's a captain. Or, it could be because "Cap" is short for his last name, Capria. No one really knew. No one really cared.

"Oh, one other thing, Jackson," Cap said.

After listening to the uncooperative motor in the Captain's throat for about 30 seconds, Jackson answered, "What is it?"

"One of the security guards is missing. The security guard that reported the bombing said the missing guard went to see where the loud bang came from and never came back. After a few minutes, there was smoke coming from the 17th floor and that's when he called the Fire Department. He hasn't seen the other guard since."

"So, you mean to tell me this sissy guard didn't even attempt to find his colleague?"

"As I said before Jackson, his statement was that after he called the Fire Department, he went to the 17th floor to see what happened and if he could find the other guard. It was too dark and slippery for him to go any further than the entrance, he said. So, he came back downstairs. Look Jackson, just get started on the case! You can find out all this extra information later!" The captain slammed the phone down without saying goodbye. He wasn't acquainted with good-byes. Jackson was used to it.

Jackson immediately called Viccers. Viccer's wife, Beverly, who was somewhat disoriented at the time of the call, answered the phone. After Jackson tried to convince her for the fourth time that he wasn't calling regarding a survey, Vic snatched the phone from his wife. "It's 3:50 in the morning, this better be good," Vic said.

"Ooh, I'm scared. If you're trying to sound tough, it's not working. Now, get up!"

"Man, are you crazy?"

"There's been a bombing in Century City. Cap wants us to get down there and check it out. I'll be at your house in fifteen minutes." Jackson hung up quickly. He knew that he didn't have time to let Vic start his usual whining and crying. If he allowed Vic to talk he would have to listen to him say things like: "Look at the time. Can't this wait until day break?" Vic's most important question, however, would be whether he had enough time to take a shower. It was too early in the morning. Jackson didn't want to listen to Vic whine for twenty-five minutes because his beauty rest was interrupted. Jackson also knew if he would just hang up the phone, Vic would get ready.

Vic's full name is Randall Viccers. Everyone at the department, however, referred to him as Vic. He is a tall, dark, chestnut complexioned, well-built young man. Jackson described his new partner to his wife, Margaret, as "one of those too-educated, too clean brothers."

"Is there such a thing as someone being 'too educated', Dale?" she asked her husband.

"You know what I mean. He's too perfect, too neat. Likes everything in order."

"Humph, the audacity of him," she responded as she laughed.

"He talks like he's white."

"No you didn't go there Dale!"

"Well, you know what I mean. He's stuffy. And Margaret, he doesn't drink any alcohol."

"For shame!"

"You know I don't like anyone who's just too darn good for a Bud."

"Sounds to me like he's cultured, educated, sophisticated and tidy. Nothing's wrong with that. He has the makings of a good husband."

"Well, he's too much of something. You know he's the type that just might be a repressed homosexual. One who is still peeking out of the closet." In the most feminine voice he could manage he said, "A dainty flower, waiting for the perfect time to blossom." Changing his voice back to its normal tone Jackson continued, "He says he's religious. I say he's a punk. Now, what do you have to say about that?"

"He's groomed," Margaret responded. "He probably is a very religious man."

"I say he's a sissy. Most of those so called saints are 'aints' anyway."

"Who are you to say who is and who isn't a saint. Do you have a heaven or a hell to put people in, Dale?"

"Nope. But I just call 'em as I see 'em. The good book says 'ye shall know a tree by the fruit it bears.' And them sissies sho 'nuf have a bunch of fruit hanging on their limbs."

"Dale, do you have to be so judgmental? It sounds like he's quite a gentleman."

"I guess. You know, he confronted me about how I said he talks like he's white. He wanted me to explain to him what it meant to talk white."

"That's good for you! You know better than that anyway. That's such an ignorant statement. Your own children have been accused of the very same thing and you were angry when they told us about it. What did you say to him?"

"I told him black folk don't talk that 'uppity' mumbo jumbo." Jackson intentionally and sarcastically began to talk the way he believes "real" black people should speak, especially those he thinks are "down-to-earth brothas." "He ack like he 'da only one know howta talk. I jest don't haf to talk 'dat way to prove myself to nobody. I knows I ain't stupid. I don't need tah put on no airs. Now, when I'm 'round 'da man, I talk 'da way he talk, if I want. He say he jest wasn't raised talkin' like 'dis heah. Dat's jest the way he talk. And since he knows he sho nuf is black, he must talk black, 'cause dats what he is. I guess he thinks he done told me a thing or two."

"Dale Cornelius Jackson! I know you didn't talk to that man like that. Did you? Now, you do sound ignorant. Do you talk to him like that often?"

"Nah. Just when I want to irritate the pants off him. It's all in fun baby. All in fun. Why, are you embarrassed?"

"Yes! And he must think you're a pretty ignorant man. Oh, and what he must think of me as well."

"He said he knows I'm an intelligent man and that I know the business well. That I'm the best detective in the business. He just doesn't understand why I haven't tried to expand my knowledge. He says a little education never hurt anybody. I told him that's true as long as people don't let their education go to their head. He asked me, 'isn't that where educa-

tion and knowledge is supposed to go, to someone's head.'
Like I said, he has a smart mouth.

***

Since Jackson's wife, Margaret didn't budge after the
phone rang or during either of his conversations, Jackson
decided not to wake her up. But, he needed a clean shirt and
some fresh socks and he didn't know where Maggie, as he
affectionately referred to her, kept them. If he tried to wake
her up, it would be an impossible and unsuccessful task.
Even if he tried to kill her. Maggie slept through the 1994
Northridge earthquake. It just passed her by. Jackson tried
to wake her up, but she didn't budge. Jackson thought
Viccers was similar to his wife Maggie. Prissy. She was
meticulous, his opposite.

He can never find his clean clothes. He remembered that
he kicked his clothes and shoes under the bed last night,
since Maggie went to sleep before him. He could be a little
lazy. He didn't have to put them in the hamper like she constantly nagged him to. So, he just put those same clothes
back on. "Ooh-Ooh-Wee!," he thought. They smelled horrible. "Okay, I won't smell fresh. I'm a man," he thought. No
sense in trying to wake Maggie just for some clean socks.
She'll kill me and I won't be able to protect the lovely City of
the Angels."

Jackson knew Vic was going to say something about the
smell in his car. 'SO WHAT!" he thought. "I'll make him

think I ate some food in the car and the smell didn't leave. He won't know it's this shirt I've worn for three days. At least not until we get out of the car and he still smells it on me." He warmed up his 67 Chevy and left for Vic's house.

Two

"Jack, why did you hang up the—O no," Viccers frowned as he covered his nose. My goodness! What is that smell?" Vic asked, as the left side of his lip touched his nose. "It smells like a hamburger with a ton of raw onions in here. This car reeks! I'm rolling down the windows. How can you sit in here and let your car emit a stench like this. This is a foul odor."

"Vic, it's cold outside, man. Roll those windows back up!"

"You're not killing me Dale and if I continue to sit in this car without ventilation I am going to die from this malodor! What is this stench?"

"Man," Jackson said quickly. "I had a double Fatburger with chilli and extra onions last night."

"What happened? I thought you and Margaret were going to Dulan's for dinner. You went to Fatburger's instead?

"Man, you know me. I was still hungry after the movie."

"This smell is starting to make my eyes water. It's like you dropped a ton of those onions on your floor somewhere. You really need to find it and clean it out, even if you don't clean up the rest of this mess in here. This is bad. I mean really bad!"

"Okay, just roll the window down, and stop whining like a woman!"

***

They reached the twin towers in Century City. There was so much smoke it looked like heavy fog. A great amount of police cars were parked in front and on the sides, and there were reporters hanging around. Blood-thirsty for any information they could suck out of the detectives.

***

The corridor had a slight decline as it lead to the room where they believed the bomb was had exploded. It was very dark and eerie. There was debris everywhere. The floor was wet with some type of sticky fluid. The substance was a bit more thick and gooey than water.

"Viccers, what do you see?" Jackson asked his partner.

"Man, I can't see a thing in here. This stench is killing me Jack! It's worse than that smell in your car."

"Quit cryin' man and ask one of those officers for a flashlight!

Before Viccers could ask one of the officers to hand him a flashlight, he stumbled over something heavy and sticky. Then suddenly, he slid into something and fell to the floor in the midst of the sticky fluid. Whatever it was.

"Vic, where's the light?!" Jackson yelled, "Vic!" There was no answer.

One of the seven officers in the corridor handed Jackson a flashlight. He turned it on. No one said a word. They just stood there for about forty-five seconds. Motionless. Their mouths opened despite the stench that crept up their nose and in their mouth.

It was like nothing any of them had ever seen. Even in movies. Parts of a body were spewed across the room. It was everywhere. There were too many pieces to number at first glance. There was an ear, it was torched, black; could have been burned during the bombing. It was stuck to the wall to the right of them. As Jackson started to bend down to move the heavy thing he felt on his left foot, he noticed it was someone's head. Not all of it. It was missing its lower jaw, its left eye, its bottom lip and of course, its right ear. It was covered with blood and parts of its brain—and, unfortunately, it was on his foot.

At that point, he noticed the security guard's body. It was decapitated and missing its right hand. It had at least forty or more holes in it, Jackson thought. It was resting next to Viccers, who looked to be dead or unconscious. As Jackson approached Viccers, he thought quickly about how he would break the news to Beverly. He walked so slowly that it seemed it took him two hours to reach Viccers. "Vic! Vic!" Jackson yelled as he bent closer to Viccers. Viccers' chest was moving. "Good, he's breathing," Jackson thought. He was relieved. "Boy, is Vic going to be hot when he sees what he's lying in," Jackson laughed to himself.

"Vic! Man, are you okay!," he asked.

Vic opened his eyes. He looked around the hall. His eyes widened. "WHAT IS ALL THIS!" he shouted.

"I bet my office looks pretty good to you right now. Doesn't it?" Jackson laughed as he offered Detective Viccers his hand. Part of the security guard's right hand was stuck to Vic's jacket. In an attempt not to alarm Viccers, Jackson tried to casually knock the hand off. However, whatever that liquid was, it was like glue. So, the effort to knock off the hand became more of a distinctive brush and wipe.

"Thanks man, but I don't need any help, I can wipe this gook off myself," Viccers told Jackson, unaware of what it was Jackson was wiping off. Jackson thought, "Okay, I'll let the smartie know what that was the next time he tries to front me."

"Jack, look over there," Vic pointed. "In the corner. There's another head. But that one is burned."

"Good and crispy, huh? But hey, at least he has all his head!"

"Everything has to be funny with you, huh Jack. You know, I think that's the only way you can handle these things. You know, bad situations like this one. Joke. Joke. Joke. This man is someone's son, brother, possibly husband and father. And you're making light of it. Can't you be serious for once. I know you've got some sensitivity in you somewhere. We've never— Well, I've never seen anything like this. And its a comedy to you. I'm going freaking crazy and you're acting like Eddie Murphy or Jim Carey over here."

"Don't lecture me Vic. I've never seen anything like this either. But, you're right, I've got to get through this somehow. Laughing is the only way I know how to get through almost anything in my life, man. If I didn't, I'd vomit or cry. Or I'd be depressed. You handle this madness the way you can. And I'll handle it the way I can. Anyway, how do you know it's a man?

"Jack—this is beginning to get a little spooky and gory. Those fingers seem to still be moving on that burned arm over there?"

"Yeah. Do you get the feeling someone's watching us?"

"There you go joking again."

Jackson saw something that Vic didn't, again. There was an eyeball stuck to the bottom part of Vic's right pocket on his shirt. Jackson knew he had already gotten on Vic's nerves, but he still wanted to pay him back for his "stuck up" attitude when he tried to help him before. He also knew if he didn't make light of this whole situation, they both would be basket cases. He had to keep Vic a bit angry and irritated or the job wouldn't get done.

"Look," Jackson said. "Over there. One ear stuck on the wall and a matching eye stuck to your shirt," he said while laughing and grabbing the eye off his partner's chest and shoving it in his face. Vic jumped up and down uncontrollably and shrieked like he never had before. "Just like a woman. Man, you can't handle anything. It's part of the body Vic. It's natural. You have two of them, man." Vic began wiping himself off. "Ain't no use in wipin'. You're just mixing the blood, brains and insides of that security guard and who ever else this is into your shirt. It's a part of you. Be happy," Jackson said with a smile. Jackson wiped his own face with a handkerchief and began to continue the process of investigating.

After standing frozen for a few moments, Vic said, "Why did I have to be the one to fall in all this? It should have been you since you think it's so funny!"

"Oh, quit cryin', man. Stuff like this happens to you because it disgusts you more than me. Now dust off and act like a man, if you can. Let's put these pieces together. You get it? You get it? Let's put these pieces together!"

"Yeah. Ha ha ha. I'm sorry that I'm speechless but your timely humor overwhelmed me."

"Look at that security guard. He's been shot. A lot. That puzzles me. How could someone have been in here to kill this guard? He didn't come up here until after the bomb went off. At least according to that security guard downstairs. And, he's obviously been shot several times. So, my dear Watson, the questions are how was he shot and who shot him? C'mon let's look around."

Vic pulled Jackson toward himself. "Hold up," he said.

"What's up man?"

"That's how. At least one of your questions is answered. Look," he said while simultaneously pointing toward the ceiling. There was a wire with some of the security guard's flesh and uniform hanging off of it. "It's a trap. You see that clear wire in front of us?"

"Nah. Where?"

"Look a little harder. It leads to those four oozies hooked up on the walls to the right and left of us. The guard must have walked into this wire, which severed his head. The touching of the wire then triggered those oozies to shoot all those holes in him. Get the feeling someone doesn't want us to investigate this murder?"

"Let's make sure there aren't any other surprises lurking around. Officer Frank!" Jackson yelled.

"Yes, Detective," the officer reluctantly uttered, shaken because of what he believed he was about to be asked to do.

"Get a squad in here immediately. We need someone to search for any traps that might have been set up in here. And listen," he said as he pulled him closer, "we don't need any more casualties. Oh, and one more thing, we need this done in no more than an hour. Understood."

"Yes sir," the officer replied.

Three

There were seven traps. They were positioned in the strangest places. One was even found in the private showers of the office. The question that mystified all of us was— Why? Why did this person, or persons, want to kill anyone who came in here? Everyone was puzzled. No one who came in the vicinity of this crime was supposed to leave with his life. It was the most horrific crime scenes their department had ever witnessed.

It was time for Jackson and Vic to start detecting. After all, that was their job. They had been waiting, it seemed an eternity, for the squad to finish and to destroy or deactivate all the remaining traps. Vic whined to one of the officers, "Officer are you sure there are no more traps remaining?"

"We went over that entire floor with a fine tooth comb, Detective. We found seven traps. Seven. If there are any more, it would be a surprise to us," he assured the nervous and shaking Vic.

"C'mon Vic," Jackson yelled. "Let's go do our job. Someone's been killed and they're probably looking up at us wondering why we aren't tying to find their killer."

"Jack, you never cease to amaze me. You're still joking like this is all fun and games. Why does the man have to be looking up at us as opposed to looking down at us. And, don't you realize that these officers are human, they could have missed a trap, you know. Humans make mistakes."

"Humans make mistakes," Jackson repeated in a girlish and sarcastic tone. "Vic, if you don't take your sorry butt up those stairs—GET UP THERE! Sorry behind. Just like a woman," he laughed. What Vic didn't realize is that his comedic partner was scared too. Just a little bit though, he wanted to think. He wasn't scared of dying, he'd say to himself. But, he knew he didn't want to watch someone else die, again. It would be a little hard for him. His first partner died, on top of him. He remembers it vividly and had nightmares about it for some time. His grandmother always told him, "Baby, every body handles things differently. Some of 'em laugh, some of 'em cry." So, from that point on he decided his way would be to laugh. The laughter disguises his true emotional need to cry. But, for now his chosen form of release is to laugh. He's well aware that Viccers thinks he is insensitive and that's fine with him. Death is so final, there are no returns. Even if there were, Detective Dale Jackson wouldn't want to greet one who recovered from the dead.

***

It was a mess. Someone really hated this man. Everything was blown, scattered, and spewed across the office. On Jackson and Viccers first case, Jackson told Viccers, "Let's see if we'll have a good day today." "Well, how do you all classify a good day around here?" Viccers asked. "A good day is when you open a door at the scene of a crime and you are able to enjoy the scenery of someone's innards. You know, you just don't know how beautiful life is until you've seen someone's innards. Simply delightful! Then you must go straight to lunch. Makes a meal taste scrumptious," Jackson replied sarcastically.

Jackson believed that someone must have severed this victim's head before the bombing occurred. A machete had to be the weapon used because of the concise cut. The deceased was Emory Payne. He was a criminal defense attorney; assisting the very wealthy residents of Beverly Hills, Bel Air, Pacific Palisades and of course, Malibu. He never lost a case. He was a suave, charming, convincing and sometimes vicious attorney.

There were no other bodies found; just Mr. Payne and the unfortunate security guard, who happened to be in the wrong place at the right time of a murder. One of the officers told Jackson and Viccers that the traps were set to go off only once and therefore the person who set them made sure that the job would be done once the trap was activated.

They contacted the dead attorney's wife, Mrs. Katie Payne, at about 9:30 that morning. As they approached the beautiful, spacious home of Mr. and Mrs. Payne, they saw a beautiful woman picking roses from the garden in the front of the house.

"Good morning," Detective Jackson said to the woman who wiped her forehead as she looked up from her garden at the detectives, shielding her eyes from the sun. Her brown hair was pulled back into a pony tail and her figure covered by a light blue denim long sleeve shirt and bleached denim pants.

"May I help you?" she asked as she took her gloves off to shake the detectives' hands.

"Yes, we're looking for a Mrs. Payne."

"And you are?"

As he revealed his badge to her, Jackson said, "I'm Detective Dale Jackson and this is my partner, Detective Randall Viccers, of the Los Angeles Police Department. Are you Mrs. Payne? If so, we're here to speak to you about your husband."

"About my husband. Is there something wrong with Emory? Is he in some sort of trouble? What's going on?"

"Take it easy Mrs. Payne."

"Take it easy. You come to me, announce yourselves as detectives, tell me that you'd like to speak to me about my husband and then tell me to take it easy. Well, that's not so easy to do."

"Could we speak further to you about this inside your home? It would make things better for us as well as you."

"Sure," she said. Mrs. Payne, who was still stooping near her flower bed, stood up and took the detectives inside her home. The entrance was classy and the decor was modern and very peachy, Detective Viccers thought. Everything was either peach or creme, with hints of black here and there. Mrs. Payne led the detectives through the entry hall, which was interrupted by a curving staircase, past the living room to a large den. A trendy African motif accented the entire room. "Have a seat gentlemen. Would you like any coffee, tea, juice or water?"

"No thank you ma'am," was Viccers' response. "We've already had a bite to eat." Mrs. Payne sat down across from the detectives. As she crossed her feet, left leg over the right leg, she then daintily placed her left hand under her right hand, and asked, "I'm trying really hard to keep my composure. So, what's going on. I'm attempting to remain calm. Is Emory alive?"

"I'm sorry Mrs. Payne, your husband was found dead in his office in Century City this morning."

"Dead. NO! Emory's not dead. This can't be happening. What happened?" she asked as she shook nervously and tears began to flow from her eyes down her cheeks.

"There were explosives. He was tied up, shot and burned pretty badly. A security guard was also killed."

"If he was burned so badly, how can you be sure it was him?"

"His head was pretty much intact and burn free. His body is another story. To confirm, we would like you to go down and identify your husband's body."

"I don't know if I will be able to do that."

"Does your husband have other family who we can have identify his body?"

"His mother could. Or his sister."

"When was the last time you spoke to your husband?"

"Yesterday afternoon before he left to go to the office. He told me he would be late."

"But Mrs. Payne, he didn't come home. That didn't concern you?"

"No. Emory has stayed out all night on numerous occasions. Especially, if he's busy on a case. This is normal."

"Even without calling you to tell you that his plans have changed."

"Yes. He wasn't always the most concerned man. But he was a good man. Will I be able to have a funeral for him. Is his body burned that badly?"

"I believe you will, he's not burned beyond recognition. Mrs. Payne this was a horrific murder. Traps were set up everywhere on the floor where your husband's office was. Evidently the killer or killers didn't want anyone to try to save your husband. From our initial viewing, he apparently died a slow death and was probably still living when the security guard came to help. Do you know of any enemies your husband might have had? Did he owe money to someone? Are you aware if any of his business deals went soar? Or, do you know why someone would want your husband dead?"

"No, no, no!" she screamed as she rocked back and forth, shaking nervously and now crying hysterically. Because she began to hyperventilate, she was no longer able to answer their questions. As Viccers went to get a cold towel, Jackson called the paramedics. The paramedics came and gave Mrs. Payne a sedative, which calmed her and she fell asleep on the couch in the den.

***

At that time there were no suspects. The detectives did consider Mrs. Payne as a suspect, momentarily. Who else would have wanted him dead? They thought. But, why would Mrs. Payne want her husband of fifteen years dead? After speaking to Mr. Payne's parents, his siblings and his secretary, they concluded that Mr. and Mrs. Payne lived a story book life. A fairy tale, not the nightmare that this incident had turned out to be.

Two days after the bombing, and after receiving absolutely no cooperation from anyone, the two detectives, during a search of the records at the home branch office of the Payne's accounts, stumbled on to something suspicious in the Payne's banking records. They went to pay the Payne's bookkeeper, Paula Daley, a visit. She cooperatively went over the books with them.

Mr. Payne had several bank accounts. Some substantial, some moderate. A portion of his wealth was dispersed in his name, his company's name only and some in both his and his wife's name. None of the accounts were in Mrs. Payne's name alone. However, Mrs. Payne was smart. She had obviously done her research. Recently. The day before the bombing occurred, to be exact, Mrs. Payne withdrew eighty-five percent of the funds from every account, which didn't require her husband's signature. There were seven accounts Mrs. Payne shared with her husband. Only one required his signature in addition to hers.

"Emory," Ms. Daley, a somewhat manly looking, yet attractive woman, who donned a tailored blue pen-striped pants suit and a short curly afro, said as she quickly corrected herself. "I mean, Mr. Payne, asked me to label each account according to its purpose: retirement fund, household expenses, family miscellaneous fund, household payroll, and Katie's personal."

"Of course," Detective Jackson said with all the confidence he could muster, because of course, he was certain the account he was about to name was correct, "Mr. Payne required his signature on the retirement account, right."

"No," Ms. Daley declared. "Oddly enough, Mr. Payne required both his and her signature on Mrs. Payne's personal account only."

Vic, looking just as perplexed as Jackson did said, "That's strange. Did he tell you why he wanted to sign on that account?"

"No. He gave no reasons; that was just his specification. She must have his signature on her personal account."

Vic, beating his partner to this next question asked, "Do you have any idea why he wanted to sign this account?"

"Well, I guess it's insecurity," Ms. Daley stated and then she began to tell a brief history of the Payne's relationship. "I think Mr. Payne was quite insecure because Mrs. Payne is attractive. She could be a nice catch for anybody. And on top of that, she's a remarkable woman. She's an intelligent, witty, and attractive woman. She's not tall. She's not short. Just average. But, when she enters a room her presence is definitely felt. It's as if she were a priceless statue. She can make heads turn and eyes stare. She walks in an erect, 'yes, I am proud of myself and I know I'm looking good' manner. She dresses exceptionally well. Very well kept. She has a nice shape too; and she doesn't mind flaunting it in a respectful way. Tastefully, you know. She's very religious also. She attends an apostolic church in Los Angeles. They're Pentecostal. You know they're known to be quite strict in their protocol and decorum. She's not very outgoing or aggressive though. Very quiet. It's funny though, once you start Katie's mouth chattering she can be quite talkative. I admire her. Look up to her, you know. See, I've known Katie and Emory since high school. Katie and I had physical education and accounting classes together. She and Emory were high school sweethearts. They've dated since tenth grade. On and off. She was happy and secure with Emory. She trusted him. But everyone else knew that Emory slept around whenever the opportunity presented itself. He really didn't deserve her. He knew it too. She's a beautiful person." She gazed outside her office window, as if she were daydreaming.

The detectives, evaluating and taking in what they just heard, didn't want to interrupt her. They waited for each other to interrupt Ms. Daley's rendezvous. Then Jackson cleared his throat as a hint and asked, "Ms. Daley, what are you trying to tell us? Could you tell us specifically why you think Mr. Payne wanted to sign on Mrs. Payne's personal account."

"He wanted to control her," Ms. Daley declared. "That's why. I received all the receipts, statements and invoices for all the other accounts. Emory never asked about them either. But he wanted to know if she bought a dress, a hat, earrings or even feminine products. Controlling. He was pitiful. She definitely had the potential to make it without him. Emory was probably scared Katie would use the money to leave him one day."

"Are you aware," Vic asked Ms. Daley, "that over the weekend Mrs. Payne withdrew approximately eighty-five percent of the funds from all of the accounts she and her husband shared?"

Ms. Daley seemed shocked. Pushing with her feet, she rolled her chair to her computer, which was connected to the Payne's bank accounts. As her fingers fervently pounded the keyboard, and her eyes scanned the screen frantically, she said, "It's gone! What was she thinking? I bet she was going to take the children and move somewhere. I don't blame her."

Vic wanted to get down to the real "nitty-gritty," so he asked Ms. Daley, "Do you think Mrs. Payne was capable of murdering or planning the recent murder of her deceased husband?"

Jackson pulled Vic to the side. "Excuse us for one second Ms. Daley, Stupid," Jackson smacked Vic. "You should have been an attorney. Asking those stupid questions. That's like asking someone at a murder trial, 'Was the deceased breathing at the time of his demise.' C'mon," he mimics, "the recent murder of her deceased husband. Stupid."

Vic tried again, "Ms. Daley, do you believe Ms. Payne was capable of murdering or planning the murder of her husband?'

"Of course not," she replied. "That's absolutely absurd." She paused and then continued, "Well, I don't think so. Not unless she found out that he was cheating on her. I guess anyone could be potentially capable of a nefarious act while in the heat of passion. But not Katie, Katie's temperament is well contained. She's mild-mannered. I've never seen her make a scene."

"Those are just the types to commit such a heinous crime Ms. Daley," Jackson replied.

"Not Katie," Ms. Daley continued. "She avoided confrontations even when they were smacking her in the face. You don't think Katie would have had anything to do with this, do you?"

"M'am, given the recent information we've obtained, she is our one and only suspect thus far. Thank you for you time. Again, I'm Detective Dale Jackson and this is my partner Detective Randall Viccers. Here's my card. If you think of anything, anything that might be helpful in solving this case, please call me." Detective Jackson shook Ms. Daley's hand.

Paula Daley hesitantly took the card and responded, "Yes, yes Detective Jackson, I will. But Katie, she couldn't have done this! She's not capable of a crime, let alone murder. Katie's a good woman. Whatever problem she may have had with Emory, she wouldn't have tried to solve it in this way. She's truly a godly woman." Vic and Jackson thanked her again, shook her hand and left the office building.

"Seems like this Daley character has the "hots" for good ole' Mrs. Payne," Jackson said laughing. Viccers nodded with a suspecting grin.

"Yeah, there's definitely something strange with that woman," Viccers replied.

"She's got issues, don't you think?"

"A lot of issues. Poor thing."

***

Jackson and Viccers went to the Payne's home again. It was located in the View Park area of Los Angeles. As they approached the door, a fairly thin elderly woman, who wore an apron, greeted them.

"Hello. May I help you?" she asked.

"Yes," Jackson replied. "I'm Detective Dale Jackson and this is my partner Detective Randall Viccers. We would like to speak with Mrs. Payne again regarding the murder of her husband. Is she in?"

"I'm sorry Detectives, she's resting right about now. She's been having a pretty rough time, trying to deal with all of this and take care of the funeral arrangements and such. She's strong but she doesn't need any more of this questioning. You'll have to come back after the funeral has taken place. She's just not up to your questioning right now."

"Betty, let them in," Mrs. Payne shouted from the inside of the house. "I'll talk with them. I want them to find who did this to Emory anyway. We all need closure from this."

"Okay. Right this way gentlemen, but remember this lady has just gone through the trauma of her husband's vicious death, you need to be careful with her," she told them.

Asking an apparently open-ended question Vic said, "Thank you Ms.?"

"Mrs. James. I'm the maid here."

"You weren't around the other day we came?"

"I guess they don't call you Columbo for nothing."

"I guess you didn't realize you weren't living with the Jeffersons," Viccers said under his breath, hoping he was only loud enough for Jackson to hear him.

"What was that Detective?"

"It's not important."

The detectives sat down in an elaborately decorated room, which had an incredible view of downtown Los Angeles. This was the family room. It wasn't as afro-centric as the den was. Mrs. Payne was sitting with a quilt covering her and a cup of tea in her hand as the detectives were seated.

"What questions did you need to ask me gentlemen," Mrs. Payne asked. "Or have you discovered something new that I should know about."

"Mrs. Payne, we must be very blunt here," Jackson stated.

"Go right ahead," Mrs. Payne responded.

"Did you want your husband dead?"

"Come again."

"Did you want your husband dead?"

How dare you," she yelled. "I never wanted to cause Em any physical harm."

"When you say 'Em', are you referring to your husband?"

"Yes. That's what I called him for short. It was his pet name."

"Mrs. Payne, your husband has been sadistically, brutally, and methodically murdered. Whoever did this wanted it badly. You want us to find his killer don't you?"

"Of course I do. But, I didn't do it!"

"Mrs. Payne, we have reason to suspect that you did," Vic informed her.

"Me! I couldn't and wouldn't hurt have ever hurt Em. We had been happily married for 22 years. What gives you the idea that I would have done this?"

Vic interjected, as if he really solved a problem, "Mrs. Payne, did you not withdraw almost all of the money you could out of your bank accounts, file for divorce, and purchase four tickets to Houston over this past weekend?"

She became fidgety. Something was wrong. They knew she wasn't telling them something. Of course, being the seasoned detectives they are, they sensed it immediately. At that point, they knew she had a motive to kill her husband and decided to take her in for questioning because they didn't know what the motive was. As Jackson began to speak, he noticed tears starting to form in her eyes. "Mrs. Payne," he asked, is there something more you need to tell us?" She stuttered and was unable to speak. The Miranda issues were taken care of with her and the detectives asked her if she wanted to speak to her attorney. She did, of course. The detectives allowed her to call and speak to her attorney privately before they left her house. They knew she needed help. She seemed gentle and they wanted to help her, but they wanted to solve this case even more.

Four

Katie Payne seemed harmless enough. Actually, she was just like Paula Daley described her. It wasn't that she was so incredibly beautiful or remarkably pretty, but her presence was definitely unmistakable. She seemed genuinely nice and gentle. She was articulate, soft spoken and statuesque in her stature. Jackson and Viccers couldn't figure out how she could be capable of committing or causing this heinous crime to be committed. However, she was the only likely suspect. The cards were all against her. She withdrew a substantial amount of money out of those accounts, she filed for divorce two days before the murder was committed, and she bought four one-way airline tickets to Houston. Obviously, she knew something was going to happen.

As she sat across from Jackson and Viccers in the interrogation room, still crying softly, they informed her and her attorney, Mozella Hemphill, of the charges against her. Jackson was getting a little sick and tired of Ms. Payne's crying. She never stopped. He thought if she did it, she should just face the music. Like his favorite statement, "Take it like a man. You did, face up to it."

Suddenly, Ms. Payne sat erectly from her slumped and slouching position. She patted her eyes and cheeks with a tissue, erasing all signs of tears. As she cleared her throat and began to speak, Jackson observed a changed and determined woman. It was as if she did a total 180-degree change. At that moment, a different woman emerged. Maybe she was capable of this murder after all, he thought.

Jackson thankfully and happily seized the opportunity of a dry moment and asked her, "Are you ready to talk to us now Ms. Payne?"

"Yes I am detective," she replied.

"Tell us your activities four days prior to your husband's murder."

"What do you want to know. Everything I've done?"

"Almost. We'd like to know, at least, what you might think could help your case and could hurt your case. Just be honest with us. We're only trying to solve this case."

"I'm thinking. I just don't know what you'd want to know. I know that I didn't kill or have my husband killed."

"The money. Tell us about it. A majority of it is gone! Why did you do it?"

"Yes I withdrew the money. I filed for divorce and bought the airline tickets. But I didn't kill Emory. And I didn't have him killed either," she stated with a voice now clear and free of nervousness. She almost appeared angry.

Jackson cleared his throat and asked, "We assume you bought airline tickets for yourself and your two children. Who did you buy the fourth airline ticket for?"

"I bought the extra one for my mother."

"Hmm, and you want us to believe that statement. Mrs. Payne you must cooperate with us if we are to solve this case and of course if we are to help you in any way. If you expect us to believe that you had nothing to do with your husband's murder, you must answer all of our questions."

"I have tried."

"Where is your father? Are your parents divorced?"

"No my parents aren't divorced and my father is still living."

"So, why didn't you buy a ticket for your father?"

"Because I just didn't want to. That's all. There was no need to buy my father a ticket. He wouldn't go anyway."

"Mrs. Payne," Viccers shouted as he pounded his fist on the table. "We can help you if you help us. But, you must be truthful with us!"

"I am being truthful."

"We have been told that your marriage was like a fairy tale," Viccers stated. "Why would you want to divorce your husband, take his family away from him and take someone else with you too? Someone whom you refuse to name."

"I don't want anyone else involved. They have nothing to do with this! What should matter most is that I didn't kill Emory! But I know a lot of women who were just as angry as I was with him right before his death."

"What?"

"Yes, I when I took that money and bought those airline tickets and filed for divorce I did so because I was angry with Emory. Many things unfolded right before this tragedy occurred."

"So you do confess to being angry with your husband. There was in fact some kind of disagreement between you," Jackson said as if he found a treasure chest.

"No, I confess to nothing. I just merely stated that I was angry with my husband. I can be angry and still not kill any one. I did not kill my husband. I wouldn't do anything like that. And the way it was done—I couldn't even imagine it. Anyway, like I said, a lot of people were angry with my husband."

"So it sounds as if you know some things we need to know. So, go on," Jackson urged her. "Tell us everything."

"I don't know where to begin."

"Begin from the beginning. We don't need to fill in any blanks or find a lot of holes. We can only help you if we know everything."

As she fought tears, she began to tell them as she shook herself as if to get rid of any pain and anguish…

"I have a group of friends," Mrs. Payne stated. "We've all known each other for quite some time now. They each knew that I've dated Emory off and on since high school. He was my first and only love. But, but, he shouldn't have done this to me." She stopped and began to shake and cry uncontrollably as she had done before.

"Mrs. Payne, you'll have to continue," Jackson said. "He shouldn't have done what?"

"Well, I found out that they knew so much more about my husband than I ever did. No one ever told me. No one. Not even Paula. Nor Rosalind. I thought they were my friends. Maybe they are. But, I felt so much pain. So much hate. So much rejection. So much confusion. So many emotions that it's hard for me to think. And the hurt Paula has gone through because of Emory, it's terrible."

"Paula Daley, right? Your accountant," Jackson asked.

"That's right. Aside from Rosalind, Paula was one of my closest friends. Anyway, Rosalind one of closest friends invited me to her office. She's a psychologist. I didn't know that this one meeting would change my life forever.

***

Five

"Hi Dana," Mrs. Payne said to the receptionist as she entered her friend, Rosalind Gayland's office.

"Oh, good morning Mrs. Payne. All the other ladies are waiting for you inside," Dana replied as she pointed to the direction of her boss's office.

Before going into the room, Katie didn't know who the other ladies were but she was aware that her friend Rosalind had invited other women to be a part of this group session. Rosalind asked several women to consider their current and/or past intimate relationships and come prepared to discuss their reactions to others when faced with negative or positive energy from their mates. In essence, she wanted to know if they went on a rampage at the office after a verbal battle with their mate that morning. Or after a romantic night of lovemaking and dinner with their mate, did they buy donuts for their entire office staff the next morning. The tentative name of Rosalind's proposed book was 'Stop Allowing Men To Control Your Life, Take Charge of Your Emotions'. Rosalind's premise was to prove that women

allow their relationships with men to affect their relationships with others."

Katie thought the session might at least be fundamentally
stimulating. Perhaps socially humorous, if nothing else. She
agreed to be a part of the group, although at first she was
quite apprehensive. Her decision was made after conversing
with her husband, Emory, about the group. He encouraged
her to be a part of the sessions. "You know how most women
are," Emory said confidently.

"No," Katie replied, "how are we?"

"Unhappy," he asserted. "Never satisfied. They want a bed
of roses, absent the thorns of course. If they find a thorn,
they'll throw the rose away." As he turned around to see his
wife's extremely bothered face he continued, "Baby, all I'm
saying is that you don't find many roses with thornless
stems. Many of them grow that way. It's the same for men.
Men are men. We will always be. We're not perfect!"

Katie looked a bit surprised now, hearing a side of her
husband she wasn't as familiar with. Except those times he
would tell her how he was glad she was more of a lady than
most women. She paused a minute before asking, "Don't
you think women should want the best? If I had to lie in a
bed of roses, I wouldn't want to get stuck with a bunch of
thorns. Sure, I could live with a few of them here and there.
Don't you think I deserve the most exquisite, colorful and
thornless roses that exist?"

"Sure you do. And you've got it," he snickered as he
winked his eye at her. Bu, it's just that even with an impec-

cably incredible specimen, such as myself," he clears his throat as he raises his eyebrows and poses in the mirror behind him, "most women would have long since found something wrong with me. They would have been looking for trouble. And when you go searching, you find."

"Em, women, or should I say people in general, don't usually search for something they don't think already exist. Just because I can't see the Big Dipper with my naked eye doesn't mean it's not out there. So," she pauses, looking at him to make sure he is listening and to evaluate his facial responses, and continues, "it sounds as if you're telling me that women should abide by that old cliché, 'what you don't know won't hurt you.' And that's stupid. Now, most of the time the issues have to do with a man cheating on his partner and she finds out. Then you men have the nerve to act shocked when she's double angry because she found that: number one, the Big Dipper has existed long before she found out about it. Number two, that her man has been hanging out with, eyeing and enjoying the company of the 'big dipper' without informing her about it. And, number three, she stumbles on her man in the clutch of those amazingly formed stars. Then, he'll say it's her fault because everything would have been 'all right' if she hadn't gone snooping and peeking around trying to spot a brother with Ms. Big Dipper. Now, that's a lot of nerve. Especially since his woman didn't create the Big Dipper. And she didn't force him to look at it or enjoy it. It was there before she knew it existed."

Emory sits for a moment, allowing what his wife just said to sink in. He is somewhat surprised because Katie, who he knows is confident, articulate and secure, is **never, ever** confrontational or out spoken about certain issues. He thought, "Boy, I must have not only touched a nerve, but I must have aggravated it pretty badly." As he scratched his head and raised his brow he thought what his next statement should be in those fast moving seconds that passed. "Just like that. Women try to plead cases of which they've gathered little or no evidence for. First of all Katie, Mr. X was more than likely just gazing at the 'Big Dipper', one of God's eye-pleasing creations; a product of nature. Men look at what pleases the eye. It's only natural. Then here comes Mrs. X, or a Mrs. X wanna be, making remarks and asking questions like, 'Do you know her? You're looking at her because you like her, don't you? I know you like her. Just say it! Say it! You like her. I can handle it. Say it! That's what you wanted all along, to be with her and not with me. Well you can have the Big Dipper. So he starts seeing the Big Dipper. Mrs. X pushed Mr. X. You see, a lot of times some women provoke a man to do certain things. All that nagging!"

"I don't nag."

"No, YOU don't. But most women do. Baby, see we're both lucky to have each other. Two happy and content individuals. All I'm saying is that I'm sure ALL of the women who will attend Rosalind's session, with the exception of you, my sweet baby, will be sourpusses. They'll have sour stories to tell, about their sour, mentally and emotionally bruised egos and hearts. And it will be mainly because they wanted perfection. If a guy shows the smallest sign of imperfection, they'll start their tongues-a-waggin', their heads to swirlin', and their fingers to pointin'."

"So, are you telling me that you don't think I should be a part of the group?"

"No. Actually, I'm saying just the opposite. I think that you might be an asset to the group. A breath of fresh air, for Rosalind's sake, of course. She'll grow weary and tired of the tales of those other women. By sharing your experience of a happy, content and fulfilling relationship, you might make the other women see that there are good relationships in the world. Especially when a woman is as great and virtuous as you are."

"Oh, somehow I think that's an insult, although I'm sure it was meant as a compliment."

"But of course. You'll tell them how you handle your relationship and any problems that might occur in it. A relationship is all about teamwork, support and understanding each other. I think your experience will benefit most of those women. You will prove to them that there are good men out there. Intelligent. Handsome. Strong. Supportive. Family-oriented men. Like me. But, that's only if those women are not so stubborn that they don't want to listen."

"Em, you're so narcissistic. You're not the best man that walked this earth you know. I just make you believe that you are."

"Yes, and that's why my relationship with you is perfect," he smiled jokingly and gave Kaite a gentle kiss on the lips and teasingly said, "I know you feel those sparks. Go on, admit it, I know you do. I see the gleam in your eye and that blush forming on your cheeks. See, I still make you want to scream. Don't I?"

After mentally reliving that "scene" as she calls it, Katie enters the room, where to her surprise she sees five women to whom she is quite familiar. There was Paula Daley, her high school and college friend and accountant. Then there is Lynette Carroll, a nurse and a high school and college friend; Theresa Johnson, her high school friend and Emory Payne's current legal secretary for ten years; and Jazmyn Hemphill, Mr. Payne's recently hired twenty-three year old legal assistant/intern. Of them all, however, Rosalind Gayland was her closest and dearest friend. Katie couldn't believe Rosalind invited these particular women to be a part of the same group with her. She wondered what made Rosalind choose them. Knowing Rosalind, as Katie did, she knew Rosalind had a motive, a reason. That there was something or some conclusion she wanted to reach by having these specific women in the same room. "That's odd," she thought to herself as she greeted everyone and sat next to Jazmyn.

"Good morning ladies," Rosalind Gayland said after everyone greeted each other. "Let's get started. I first want to briefly explain to you why I've asked you here. I am conducting a survey about relationships and their effect on women's minds, bodies and spirits. I want you, when asked, to speak specifically and explicitly about your relationships. The more honest you are, the more effective and accurate my survey and analysis will be. I first want you all to discuss your best relationship, which you can also say turned out to be your worse. I don't want any of you to interject while someone else is speaking. There are pads in front of you. You can take notes while others are sharing their experiences. We will have a group discussion after everyone has spoken. Okay, let's begin with you, Lynette. Describe to us your best relationship, which is actually your worse one and why.

***

Six

Lynette Carroll

"Well, Rosalind," Lynette says jokingly, "that's going to be hard. Especially since I know everyone here, except Jazmyn. But, I'll try. The relationship I had that best fit that description was during high school. Well, in a way, it continued well beyond high school."

"High school!" Theresa screamed as she adjusted her sunglasses. "Girl, you weren't dating anyone in high school. High school! It's that fella you met during college that knocked you up that you should be talking about. Not some boy in high school. I knew you. You kept your legs as tight as sardines in a can while we were in high school. It's the boy you let open that can in college that got you in trouble."

"Theresa!" Rosalind shouted. "I said no interruptions during someone else's turn. Now SHUT UP girl! And I mean that professionally."

"Well, telling me to 'shut up girl' is not very professional," Theresa said, who is quite an intelligent and articulate woman, except when she's around her "running" buddies she tends to change to "street" vernacular. Everyone also knew that Theresa is all bark but no bite. "And you also said that we should be truthful because you would get a better outcome on your survey. I'm just trying to help a sistah out here. And look at the response I get."

"What you should do Theresa is take off those sunglasses, put your purse down and relax. You're in the presence of friends. Now, we will let Lynette continue," Rosalind said.

"Well, I started dating him in high school. He actually had a girlfriend during high school but he had broken up with her when we started dating. Then, while I was in college, I'd still see him from time to time. He said he was going to break up with his girlfriend because she wasn't a real woman. He said she acted like a child in many ways. She told him she would not consummate their relationship until he married her. I was young. A high school girl who wanted to have fun and experience what everyone talked about. I gave him my virginity during the beginning of our twelfth grade year.

"Anyway, he'd buy me things. And even though he was with her in high school, he'd blink his eye at me when she wasn't looking. I felt special. She was so pretty and popular, and he said he liked me more than her. That I was more like a woman and that I was sensitive to his needs, unlike her. I had fallen in love with him. So, we continued to see each other on and off. And he continued to make the promise that we'd someday be a pair. And I fell for the lies. I was blind.

"During my second year in college, I got pregnant with his baby." Lynette then stares out the window of Rosalind's office. A tear drops on her skirt. She takes the tips of both her middle fingers and wipes each eye simultaneously. That's when everything changed," she recalls.

"You're what!" he screamed.

"I'm pregnant," I said. "With our baby. Our first baby!"

"You're not pregnant with my baby. Who have you been seeing?"

"I don't see anyone but you. You were my first and only. I've always been faithful to you. I don't have anybody else!"

"Stop lying. You're just another whore out to get something!"

"Whores don't accidentally get pregnant. They make sure they can still work."

"Okay then. You admit it, you got pregnant on purpose. You just thought you'd make me leave my girlfriend and run off and have a family with you, huh? You're no good. You're just like the rest of them"

"The rest of them! How many are there?

"Look, I have to finish school. I don' have time for a baby. You should have been taking care of yourself. What's wrong with you?"

"I think this happened when I told you I wasn't ready. Remember?"

"Don't try to blame this mistake on me! You're the woman, you should have been taking care of your own business!"

"My own business. You told me you loved me. You told me you were going to break it off with her and one day marry me. Don't you remember any of those things you promised me?"

"Promised you. Stop being so naïve, Lynette. There's no woman better than my girl. I could never leave her. I would never marry you! You should have always known that."

"So what was I to you? What is this baby to you?"

"Well first, you were a friend who I was having fun with. And this baby…this baby is a mistake. This baby is nothing because you're going to have an abortion. You need to finish school and I'm going to finish school without that hanging over my head!"

"When I told him I was not going to have an abortion, he told me that he already decided that he was going to marry his girlfriend. That he couldn't break up with her after all those years. And, that I should get the abortion and go on with my life.

"While I thought I was in the happiest and best relationship ever, I was actually in the worse. I just couldn't see clearly. As you all know, I gave birth to Tiffany. He visits her now and sends her presents and money. After he finished school, he tried to see that she was okay. He said he always felt guilty that I had to stop college and support her. So, that's how I finished school after she was four years old, he provided daycare for her, bought my books, and gave me spending money from time to time. He's been okay. I've slipped with him a few times after he got married. But, after two years into his marriage, I woke up. I told him I couldn't do this with him any longer. His wife was my friend. I felt terrible enough. I tried to convince myself that his wife would understand that our relationship didn't start until they were broken up in high school. When they got back together, he stopped seeing me. Then in college, we got back together during one of the times they were broken up. That's when Tiffany was conceived. Anyway, he'd threaten to stop supporting Tiffany. I threatened to tell his wife if he didn't stop pursuing and pressuring me. See he'd do all the calling and writing.

"Then when I started dating other men, he stopped giving me money for Tiffany for a while. He wanted to control me. It was really hard for me financially during that time. I didn't have a degree and I didn't have any skills. I was desperate. So, I threatened to tell his wife about Tiffany if he didn't help me. So, he helped me until I finished school. Now, Tiffany is 18 and in college. He's just helping her with school and with her other necessities. And that's fine with me. I don't really want him in my life anyway. I am glad that Tiffany knows who he is and has been able to maintain a relationship with him despite his other family.

"Well, as you all know, I finally graduated from college and started working as a registered nurse at Cedars Sinai. That gave me a more meaningful career, a more substantial income to support my daughter and myself without his assistance. I took care of Tiffany and myself without needing his help and I have absolutely no interest in him. Especially since I know he continues to cheat on his wife—and it's not with me! I mean, I'm not happy that he cheats on his wife, but it reminds me that I wasn't special to him. That it's good I'm not in that stupid affair. And, that he's simply a D-O-G!—and I'm not missing out on anything. I feel quite free now. I've been in his presence recently and I don't feel a thing for him. As long as he treats my daughter right, I'm okay. And, fortunately, she doesn't look noticeably like him. So, I'm not constantly reminded of him when I look at her." Lynette dabs her tear-stained cheeks with one of the Kleenex tissues Rosalind gave her and settled back in her chair. The room was quiet for a while and Rosalind broke the silence.

"Are you finished?" Rosalind asked Lynette.

"Yeah, that's about it. Ros, you know the story. I've cried on your shoulders many times. Although I haven't really revealed much to all of you, I feel much better now that I have shared this will all of you. And, since the other information I've shared with Rosalind is privileged, she won't disclose those facts. I feel good. As you all know, I'm now engaged to Richard, one of the doctors at the hospital. Tiffany likes him and he thinks the world of her. We treat each other with respect and we have a lot in common.

"To answer your survey question, Ros; yes, for many years that one relationship effected me so negatively that I haven't had a serious relationship until recently with Richard. I had to do a lot of growing. I was tired of being hurt. So, for many years I sulked. I delved into personal pity parties and vowed never to give my love to another man. But, during that time I did learn to love myself and come to terms with my situation. This has allowed me to have the relationship I now enjoy. I'm happy!"

"Who is that other man? You can't have a juicy relationship like this and keep the facts from your friends. Girl, I wanna know who the man is!" Theresa chided.

"That's not what we're here for Theresa," Rosalind interjected. "Anyway, any revelations should, can, and most likely will be made after everyone has spoken. Now, since you're so eager to talk Theresa, talk. It's your turn!"

***

Seven

Theresa Johnson

"Well I've know this man for years," Theresa confessed. "I guess, just like Lynette. He's good looking. He's intelligent. But, like Lynette's man, he's married too. I guess everybody's got a married man," she laughs, attempting to hide the pain. "Anyway, I didn't start dating him until long after we knew each other. He just started to excite me—even though I knew he was married. I didn't have an interest in him until he started complimenting me continuously, buying me flowers, sending me notes with the words, 'just to say hi,' written on them. Girl, he cast a spell on me. He was after me like a bee after its Queen. I resisted for at least a year. Then, his pursuits won. He's a charmer.

"I'm sorry Rosalind," Katie countered jokingly. "You know I hardly speak or interrupt, but I can't pass up this opportunity. Theresa, this explains why no one ever sees you with a man. You never have a date at my parties. I've tried to get Emory to find someone for you. But, he always tells me to stay out of your business. And you, you always tell me that you live without men. That you're a 'strong and confident woman who doesn't need to have a man in her life to justify her existence.' But, a married man. Shame on you! You're so pretty, you can have any man out there you want. Emory has said it thousands of times. That's why he told me to leave you alone, because you must like it that way."

"Well," Theresa continued after Katie's scolding. "I never though I'd fall for a married man. Girl, you know. I mean, I know his wife. But, he just sweet-talked me. Charmed me. He made me think he was going to leave his wife and be with me. Anyway, my mother keeps telling me, 'Theresa, they rarely ever leave their wives, and you're going to end up hurt and stripped of all your pride cause you did what you did, and you ain't gonna get nothing in return. Nothing.' But, I keep hoping despite my mother's warnings. She's right though. He wants me only long enough to satisfy his thrills and that's all. I'm sure he'll drop me if his wife ever got wind of our relationship. I know he loves her. I can tell.

"I guess I've been hoping and dreaming that he will some day feel for me as he feels for his wife. He talks about her often. That he's lucky to have her. But she doesn't excite him like she used to. He says she's a good mother and an excellent wife. But he's going to leave her someday. I just don't know when. Anyway, he's been acting distant with me for about three months now. I don't see him twice a week like I've been used to for the past seven years. He's always busy lately. I know there's someone new in his life. I know it. And,

I know he doesn't all of a sudden feel some fidelity to his wife. We haven't been together for three months.

"So, yesterday, I approached him. I wasn't pretty. I called him late one night at his office."

***

"Hello," he answered the phone in his deep sexy voice.

"Hi," I answered softly.

"Yeah," he said abruptly.

"I just called because I wanted to know why you haven't been around to see me lately and why you haven't called."

"I see you."

"I mean our weekly rendezvous. You haven't been by lately. What's going on?"

"Things change."

"What does that mean?"

"Changes have been made."

"Changes have been made? You sound as if you're talking about a house or some document. Why are speaking in code? Is your wife there?"

"No."

"Have you lost interest in me? Are you going to be loyal to your wife from now on? Did I make you mad or something? What is it?"

"That's it."

"What's it?"

"Yeah, that's it."

"Are you talking to me? Who's there with you? What are you doing?"

"I have to let you go."

"No. Stop being so short with me and answer my questions!"

"Okay."

"Okay! Then which is it?—Hello! I asked you a question!"

"I know."

"What's that light grappling noise I hear? Is that moaning? Is that another woman? Who is she? There's more than me!"

"That's right! Much more!"

***

"I hung up the phone. That was last night. I cried all night. That's why I'm wearing these shades, Rosalind. My eyes look terrible with them off. My eyes are blood shot and puffy, and my heart is hurting. I knew he was with his wife. But others—I didn't know. Like, Lynette, I thought I was special. That it was me he found so attractive and irresistible. He always flattered me. And you know how we can fall for that stuff.

"So, you know me, I couldn't just leave well enough alone. I was going to confront him and his little harlot. The slut. First, I picked up a bottle of Hennessey from my cupboard. And I drank, sobbed and thought. Drank, sobbed and thought. And I planned his murder in my mind. How I would kill him and her. Slowly. Then I straggled down to my car. Got in. Blasted my music. Turned on the ignition and swerved 90 miles an hour down Crenshaw Boulevard, and headed to his office building. Next thing I know, I heard this loud noise. But I kept driving despite the fact that the noise was killing me. And it wouldn't stop. It kept screaming, louder and louder. Then these red and blue bright lights start flashing. It was the police. They pulled me over."

"Ma'am. Good morning," the policeman greeted me.

"Good morning officer," I managed to say quite soberly.

"Did you know you exceeded the speed limit at about 60 miles and you're swerving?"

"I'm sorry officer. I have a lot on my mind."

"Well, maybe you shouldn't be out at this time of night by yourself."

"That's a good idea. I should just drive home."

"Have you been drinking?"

Me?"

"Yes ma'am. You."

"Well, I drank a little bit."

"Would you slowly step out of your vehicle."

"What?"

"Slowly step out of your vehicle."

"I was at the police station until six o'clock this morning. They let me go after they pushed thousands of cups of coffee in me. Kenny, that's the officer, said he thought I was too pretty to worry over sorry men. He didn't want me to get in any trouble, so he just helped me get sober and let me go.

"But now that I think about my situation again, the anger is starting to rage all over me as if someone poured a pot of scolding tar on my chest and it's slowly trickling down the rest of my body. I mean, how could he do this to me? But, I'll be okay. After I leave here, I'm going to my mother's house and cry some more. She'll make me feel better. And she won't tell me she told me this would happen, until about three months from now after she thinks I feel better.

"Men are dogs," Theresa said as she gazed in Jazmyn's direction. "See, you're young, Jazmyn. You should learn from our mistakes. You told me about your relationship with that cute young man you're seeing. What's his name? Uh, Darcel or something?" As Jazmyn shook her head in agreement, Theresa said, "Yeah, Darcel. You said that you're happy because he is a minister at your church, a devout Christian. Well, just be glad you have a nice, religious boyfriend who is devoted to you and you only. You told me about that man who has been making advances toward you. Leave him alone. Remember the old cliché, 'All that glitters isn't gold.' Stick with the man you already know is good for you and to you.

"I've learned one lesson—you have to make a man treat you right from the beginning because he'll never change."

"Okay," Rosalind whispered. "We've heard from Lynette and Theresa. How about you, Jazmyn, would you like to speak now?"

"No," Jazmyn responded softly. "I'd like to listen for a bit longer."

"I'll speak now," Katie stated.

"Well, Katie you're married," Rosalind offered. "I would like you to be last, since you've probably had a different experience than most of us. Okay?"

"Sure," Katie answered. "I'll wait."

"Let's see," Rosalind said as she shuffled the papers on her lap. "Paula. Why don't you tell us your experience next."

Eight

Paula Daley

"My experience with men. Men. I know you all think that I am a lesbian. And I thank you for remaining my friend despite the fact that you think I'm gay. I'm not dumb. I've heard all your whispered comments and I understand. But, hopefully after I've explained to you my experience with men, you will understand why I am the way I am. It happened during my first year in high school. I was skipped two grades and started high school at 13 years old.

"The rain poured and poured," Paula said, her head hanging slightly. "The clouds were smoky gray. It was early in the morning and it appeared as if nightfall was rapidly approaching," Paula continued in her usual dramatic way of speaking. "The rain came down so hard that day. It seemed as if God were angry at the universe. I was scared. I was in incredible pain and it was apparent to me that the world was coming to an end. My mother and stepfather came to pick me up from the nurse's office at school at about 10:15 that morning. I had been vomiting and cramping the entire morning. I was cold and shivering. Then the blood started to gush from between my legs as we walked to the car. I was frightened.

"My mother was crying uncontrollably. Both she and my stepfather seemed to know what was wrong with me long before I had even the slightest idea. At first I couldn't understand why they seemed angry at me. I was hurting, bleeding and dying, I thought, and they weren't attempting to comfort me.

"And then it was time for me to understand."

***

"The child is only fourteen, Constance. Fourteen," my stepfather said to my mother. "This is your fault!

"My fault," my mother yelled to my stepfather. While trembling and bleeding profusely, I listened to them argue. I was confused. They weren't concerned about my health. Their only concern was to whom the blame should be placed.

"Yes your fault," my stepfather asserted. "If you never allowed Paula, a fourteen year old, to be skipped to the tenth grade, this wouldn't have happened. My goodness, the child already looks like she's about seventeen. She's tall, built like a woman. What did you expect."

What happened was my question. What are they talking about? I'm sick. Sick! I was, as I felt then, on my deathbed. What did being skipped have to do with my illness?

"Don't blame this on me Gerald Dalton," my mother said as she fought her tears. "My daughter is extremely intelligent. It would have been a hindrance on her educational growth to stagnate her by keeping her on a level to which she had already exceeded. Anyway, many young people are skipped. We're dealing with another issue here."

"Well, Constance, they don't look like your daughter Paula."

"What does Paula look like, Gerald?"

"Look at her chest, Constance. Look at her height, Constance," he stopped the car and threw his hands in the air and his dark chestnut colored face turned burgundy. "Constance! Wake Up! Wake Up! Paula has the figure of an adult woman who works out everyday."

"That's because she's athletic. Anyway, I make her wear a sweater to cover herself everyday. Even if it's hot, she's told to wear that sweater. And she just went to high school two years early. Not five. You act as if I sent her off to college or something. Bad boys did this to *my daughter*, not me!"

"It's like you placed a fresh slab of beef in a lion's den Constance. Those boys are hungry."

My mother started wailing again and my stepfather began driving. My mother turned her head and glanced over at me from the front seat. Then she shook her head and glanced over at me from the front seat. Then she shook her head as it hung down. They seemed disappointed in me. But why? I guess I was in too much pain to logically deduce the problem.

"We're God-fearing Christians, Constance," my stepfather told my mother. "I'm the assistant pastor. You're the missionary president. We've raised Paula right. When did this happen?"

"I don't know Gerald," my mother said between sobs. "I don't know. I thought I kept a watchful eye on Paula. We've talked about this many times."

"Well, she just might lose her life over this," my stepfather said as he began to cry. "What did we do wrong?" I knew he loved me. He loved me as if I were his own child. They found out after they married that my mother could not have any more children. I was to be his only child. My father died two months after I was born. My stepfather was a deacon at the church and he started dating my mother when I was about a year old. He's the only father I knew. Like I said, I knew he loved me, but I had never seen him cry. This made me feel terrible.

"We failed her, I failed her," he said as he wiped his eyes and drove off.

"What did I do wrong?" I asked my parents as I too began to sob.

"Paula," my mother said softly, "you aren't aware of what's wrong with you?"

"No Mom," I answered. "What's wrong with me?" I asked in my innocence or stupidity. I was raised in a strict household. I really wasn't aware of many things. I was naïve.

"You're pregnant," my mother responded. "The school nurse concluded that after she examined you. You're already too far along sweetie."

"But I didn't let them finish mom. I screamed! I stopped them, mom, I…

***

"Hey," the twelfth grader said to me. He was cute and popular. I felt a bit flattered that he was speaking to me. "It's Paula, right?"

"Yes," I said as I changed my voice to sound as if I was older.

"I'm Nathan Landers, senior, varsity basketball," he sad as she extended his hand for mine. "You can call me Nate for short."

"Nice to meet you Nate."

"I see you have a lunch. You wanna eat your lunch with me on the benches behind the gym? It's real nice back there."

I felt I was big enough to have lunch with him. So I said, "Sure."

It was really cool that day and there was a subtle breeze. I sat down and began to open my lunch. And it began. He stroked his hand across my face. He looked deep in my eyes and said, "You sure are pretty. You're the prettiest girl at this school. These other girls look like girls, but not you. You look like a woman. Even in all those clothes and that sweater you wear everyday; all us guys can tell that you have it going on under there."

I smiled. Then suddenly I started feeling things tingle and it started to get really hot out there. I wanted to take my sweater off but my mother told me to keep my sweater on, especially when I'm around boys. I just did what she told me because I remembered being told that disobedient children live half their days. I couldn't understand why I had to keep that hot sweater on at all times. But it surely was getting hot out there even though there was a nice breeze.

"Loosen up," the senior varsity basketball player said. "Get comfortable. Here, I'll help you take this old sweater off. You're too pretty to hide under this sweater." As he took my sweater off, two other guys came from the side of the gymnasium.

They stood there, staring. As I searched to find the spot on my body where their eyes were positioned, I realized that they were ogling at my chest. I then became extremely uncomfortable. I felt naked. And that's when I knew why my mother wanted me to keep my sweater on. Nathan grabbed me and began to kiss me on the lips. Then he touched my upper thigh. I bit his lip and he jumped back from me.

"Man, she bit me," he screamed. That's when one of the three tore my blouse and bra off. I stood there. Motionless. Helpless. Scared. I didn't know what to do. I couldn't even scream. I was frightened. Then, that same guy pushed me on the grass, on my back and held my hands down, Nathan held my legs down and spread them apart, and the third guy kneeled down and pulled my underwear off. He then stood up and unzipped his pants. I looked at him and started crying. I guess I thought he would have sympathy for me. As he abrasively thrust himself in me about three times, I screamed from the pain, "Stop! You're hurting me. This hurts." But he wouldn't stop. I was in pain. It hurt and I kept crying uncontrollably. Then, one of the other guys yelled, "Come on man, it's my turn," as he tried to move his friend."

I looked down at myself and saw that I was bleeding. I cried hysterically, "I'm bleeding! Stop!" They all looked down at me and the one who was just on me said, "Nate, I thought you told me she'd been around. She's a virgin, man! A virgin!"

"I'm only thirteen," I cried as I struggled unsuccessfully to get up, but they were still holding me down. "Leave me alone!"

"Thirteen," the same guy who just finished wailed. "Thirteen! Look I'm sorry. They told me you were used to three of four guys at a time. I didn't mean to do this," he said. "I'm outta here, man!" He ran off. The other two looked down at me and ran right behind him. I was hurting and scared. I didn't think I could get pregnant. He only moved on top of me a few times and then it stopped; at least I thought. Although I cramped and bled for the rest of the day, I didn't think they hurt me internally. I had just started having my period a month before that happened, so I thought that incident made it come early.

I couldn't tell my mother. I felt too dirty. I just couldn't! I felt ashamed and disgusting. I thought that was going to be the end of it. I would keep my sweater on and eat lunch in the cafeteria from then on, I told myself. Anyway, the guy who did it was very nice to me after that. He kept apologizing. If other guys bothered me, he'd stop them. He wrote me a note apologizing for everything and begging me to never tell anyone. He seemed really genuine. I chalked it up as a terrible experience and tried to ignore it. I just left them alone. In any case, I was too embarrassed to mention the incident to anyone. I never told a single soul. Not until that day at the hospital.

***

"What!" my stepfather yelled. "Those no good for nothing scums. You were raped by a gang of boys and you didn't tell me or your mother?"

"I couldn't tell you," I said. Still naïve I said, "And I wasn't raped. I stopped them. It only happened once. I couldn't be pregnant. I didn't let them finish. I stopped them, mom. I really did. It hurt and I didn't like it. I was scared and I started bleeding. Then they got scared. So, it didn't happen long enough."

"Paula," my mother began, "have we sheltered you so much that you don't know all it takes is really one time. He was ready for you! Why didn't you tell me? Why didn't you report those nasty boys? Do we scare you that much?" My mother cried and things were never the same.

I had to have an emergency surgery. I didn't know why for sure. My mother didn't tell me until I asked her after about six months why I hadn't had another menstruation. That's when she told me that I would never have another period. That the boy caused actual damage to my insides. Well, I had to have a hysterectomy. My mother had to tell me, her only child, that I could not give birth. Ever. So, my mother and stepfather understood, to a degree, why I didn't want to prosecute the boys. I wanted to forget everything. They let me try. I haven't. I wish I did because I suffer every day now.

It didn't really hit me until years later. After Jason. You all remember him. We dated for about three years. His family went to our church for a while, Katie. Unlike other guys, Jason never, ever tried to touch me. He was a gentleman. He said he loved me. And, that he would love me always no matter what. He said he didn't think he could ever live without me. So, he asked me to marry him. I was elated. However, I knew I had to be honest with him. So, I told him. I told him that I had been raped when I was 13 and that the force and violence of the incident caused me to lose the ability to ever become pregnant. I thought he would be understanding and sensitive. But, he retracted his hand in marriage after I told him that I could never bear children. Not his nor anyone else's for that matter. He never spoke to me again. Stopped talking to me—cold! I absolutely hate men!

"But, to answer all of your questions regarding my sexuality—No, I am not a lesbian. I just dress the way that I do because I don't want a man to become interested in me now that I am damaged goods. I don't want to be hurt. I don't want to get married and desire children. I just want to be left alone."

***

Everyone sat quietly, wiping their tears as they each gave their friend Paula consoling hugs. It was one of those moments during the session. Although she shared in shedding tears, Jazmyn did not hug Paula. She sat there, motionless.

The silence lingered for about two minutes and the sessions continued.

Nine

"Now I understand," Katie spoke out, abruptly interrupting their silence. "That's the reason you didn't come to church for about three months. Everyone thought you were deathly ill or something. But, I still don't understand a few things. I've known you all for quite some time and you've held some major secrets from me. Why would you allow these men to do what they've done to you and get away with it? You are all intelligent women. You're not dumb! What did these men do to captivate and control your minds like they did?"

"Well," Lynette answered. "I didn't know that he wasn't the kind, gentle, responsible, godly man I thought he was—until he started to making little statements around me like, "women make a man do certain things because they nag so much."

Katie laughed, "Emory must not be the perfect man I think he is because he just said the same thing to me." She giggled a little more, recalling what he had recently said to her, "that's cute."

"Cute! You better open up your eyes, that sounds like the guy I'm seeing," Theresa said. "He told me, 'Women want a perfect man. He can't have any flaws. That's the problem, men are human. We make mistakes."

Katie laughed even harder and said, "Emory said that too. Oh, wait until I tell him he's just like any other man. You know he thinks he's God's gift."

"Of course he's like any other man," Lynette said. "The ones who aren't any good. There are brothers out there who are good men. Real men. Loving men who take care of their wives, their children and their homes. Black men who know the value of a good Black woman. Those men do exist. But you have to know how to spot them. Unfortunately, spotting them is just like picking the best watermelon. Just when you think you're good at picking the ripest, juiciest and sweetest one, you open it and bite into a section that's horrible and leaves a bad taste in your mouth. First, you bite the watermelon and you think it's okay. It's a little sour, but you can still enjoy it; you think. Just like men. They'll have you going for a while. Then you bite into a section that's so hard that you can't eat it any more, or so soft you have to spit it out. But, then you find one like Richard. He's a good black man. And girl, you know I've cut him open all over. He's not too hard—just firm enough. And, he's not so sweet that he's dripping with sugar in his britches. I'm sure I've got a pretty good melon this time."

"I know," Rosalind interjected. "Actually, I can release some of my past also. I've had my share of bad relationships. I've known all of you since high school. But I was very quiet. So, I didn't socialize with any of you then. I didn't really get to know you all until I began my professional career, especially you Katie. I saw you in high school and in college but we never really spoke. Anyway, men try to hold on to you with their sweet talk. If I told you some of the things the guy I used to date would tell me. That's the reason I started dating him because he was a smooth talker. Then, I got to know his wife really well. I started to really like and respect her. But, then I got pregnant. He wanted me to have an abortion. I couldn't. I just couldn't. So, I didn't. I went to stay with my Uncle George who lived alone in Barkersfield. Then, my baby's father came to visit me and convinced me to give the baby up for adoption. My Uncle was devastated. He told me that he would help me raise the baby if I kept it. Actually, I think he bonded with the baby for those first few weeks. I had a baby girl. She was so cute. I didn't want to give her up. So, she wasn't adopted right away. I named her Roselyn and I kept her for about two months. I breast fed her and loved her. And Uncle George woke up during the middle of the night to feed her. Then, her father came back again and forbade me to keep her. He said it wouldn't be fair to her, to me, or to his new wife. This decision was in everyone's best interest. At the time I agreed. I didn't want my little girl to know that she was conceived out of wedlock and to a father who rejected her. That her mother and father were adulterers. I wanted her to be happy. And she would be happy not knowing either of her parents; at least her father. But, knowing me would have given her access to her father. Yes, it was best to give her up for adoption. My Uncle George wanted to kill him. That was about 22 years ago. My Uncle George hasn't talked to me much since then. I am not allowed to go to his house any longer. Yet, recently he has asked me to visit him.

"After my daughter was gone for about a week, my eyes were opened. I came back to work and I found out that I wasn't important in his life because he had other women anyway. So, when I decided to end our affair he told me, 'women want a bed of roses, without the thorns, of course. If they find a thorn they'll throw the rose away. That's wrong. They won't let a rose be a rose in its natural beauty; with its thorns. Roses have thorns! Rosalind just let a man be a man. With all his thorns,' he said. That was it for me! So, I left him to his wife and his many others. It's been about twenty years now and…"

Katie stood up quickly. She trailed across the room as all ten eyes were on her. Everyone was quiet. Tears began forming in her eyes as she paced near the window. She shook her head and her right finger and said, "Wait a minute, Rosalind," as she stopped in front of her. "We've known each other now for almost thirty years, right?"

"Right."

"We've been close, almost like twin sisters, for going on about 16 years, right?"

"That's right Katie."

"I've known all of you, except Jazmyn, since junior high school. But you and I Rosalind, I thought we cared about each other like family. I want you to be honest with me. Will you?"

"All right, Katie, I will."

"Okay. Emory said the same thing to me recently that your secret man said to you. You know, about the roses. I understand that at the time you were with this man and had the baby, we were not friends. So, now be honest. Was Emory the man you dated and had a baby by years ago?"

After a silence that seemed to span a lifetime, with all eyes on her, Rosalind answered very solemnly, "Yes."

"Yes!," Theresa screamed as she stood up, hands on her hips. "Yes! I've been opening my heart to you for fifteen years now. Fifteen years and you just said yes!"

"Calm down Theresa," Rosalind pleaded. "Calm down."

With tears in her eyes Katie agreed, "Yes, Theresa calm down. Why are you getting so uptight? Emory's my husband. He cheated on me. Not you!"

"You're right," Theresa said softly. "Emory is your husband. But, I guess your friend Rosalind broke up with Emory right after I told her that he was the man I was having an affair with during one of our sessions about twenty years ago."

"WHAT! I can't believe this," Katie cried out as her eyes seemed to bulge from their sockets.

"Well," Paula solemnly added, "I can't have any children because of what Emory did to me. Because of Emory and his friends, I hate men to this day. But Emory was the one who actually did it to me. Katie, you thought Emory was just being generous by paying me this high salary. No, it's guilt. What a great reward for my loss! But, I never ever slept with Emory. Or anyone else. Never! I never tried to hurt you. I love you Katie. You're special to me. You have been my friend. I never thought I should bother you by telling you."

"Paula," Katie said as she began to shake," this can't be happening to me. I really can't believe this!"

"No," Lynette said as tears began to fall from her eyes to her lap. "I can't believe this crap either. Emory is my daughter, Tiffany's, father, …"

Katie's mouth hung open as she fell to the floor. She stayed there for about eleven minutes—motionless and slouched over the couch. As Rosalind, Theresa, Lynette and Paula continued to argue, Jazmyn Hemphill quietly left the room. With all of the hormonal energy flying around, no one noticed she left. Suddenly, they all looked at Katie, who was now sitting inertly on the floor. They then looked at each other. Katie began to move and look around. As they all looked at each other, they realized that Katie was really the one who was betrayed. Her eyes were closed; theirs were open. She's the one who slept with a STRANGER, although he was an unknown stranger. They knew him. She didn't. Simultaneously, as if they were each in tune with one another, they all gathered next to Katie on the floor. Suddenly, as if a crying child were beckoning her to save him, Theresa stormed out of the room.

***

Ten

Detective Jackson peered out of a station window. He slowly sat down across the table from Mrs. Payne, cleared his throat and tapped a pencil on the table. "So," he said as the tapping continued as he spoke. "Are you suggesting that this Theresa…" he said as he touched his nose with his right hand and then waved it to the side of his face and shook his head with a frown of curiosity on his face suggesting that he wanted Mrs. Payne to complete the name.

"Johnson, Theresa Johnson," Katie assisted the detective.

"Yes, this Theresa Johnson," he said as he wrote her name on a small pad, "your husband's secretary, committed the murder?"

"No, Detective Jackson. I'm just saying that I didn't do it. And, I'm letting you know what happened right before the murder. It could have been anybody. You can subpoena Rosalind and get the statement's everyone made. Rosalind recorded the session."

"Do you think Theresa Johnson killed your husband?" Viccers asked.

"I don't think Theresa would or could kill a flea without feeling an enormous amount of guilt," Katie admitted. "The guilt would kill her."

"Guilt didn't stop her from giving her all to your husband," Jackson countered as Viccers gave him a look that said you unsympathetic scum. "I'm mean, excuse the blatancy but isn't this the same Theresa Johnson who had an affair with your husband for almost eleven years and **that** guilt hasn't killed her yet."

"Well," Katie replied, "I just don't believe any of those women would have killed Emory. They just weren't faithful friends. They were strangers who I happened to know."

"Oh," Viccers said sarcastically, "none of them could have done it?"

"Well," Katie responded. "I don't know Jazmyn very well. But, she didn't admit to having had an affair with my husband. So there's no reason or motive for her to have done anything like this.

"Mrs. Payne, let us decide whether there is a motive," Jackson interjected.

"Well, at this point I don't know what or who to believe. And I don't know her; but I still don't think she would be capable of killing anyone. And to do it the way it was done. Someone would have to have intense anger to have done this."

"Mrs. Payne, we are going to question each of these women. They will be subpoenaed. However, we must continue to detain you."

"But, the funeral is tomorrow," Katie contested. "And my children. What's going to happen to them?"

"I will make sure you are permitted to attend your husband's memorial services," Jackson stated. "Unfortunately, we will have to escort you. Your children. How old are they?"

"Courtni is sixteen and Emory Jr. is fifteen," she answered.

"Well, their old enough to understand this," Jackson added. "Do you have someone who can stay with them?"

"Yes, my mother" Mrs. Payne said softly as she rested her head in the palms of her hands.

Viccers cleared his throat and asked, "Would you like to make those calls now or do you need time alone?"

"Um," Katie said as she also cleared her throat, "Can I have a few minutes alone?"

"Sure, Mrs. Payne," Viccers agreed. "We'll leave for a few minutes."

Eleven

Jackson and Viccers escorted Mrs. Payne to her husband's funeral. She had been arrested for suspicion of murdering her husband of 20 years. Since Mrs. Payne had no prior record, Cap saw no need to put handcuffs on her during the service or in front of people.

The funeral was baffling. There were too many people to count. Actually, ninety-five percent of the people who attended Mr. Payne's funeral were females. Young women. Ranging between the ages of 20 and 40. All of them were beautiful. They all also were seemingly happy and inappropriately smiling; almost on the verge of giggling. The remaining people were his family and about seven men who stuck out of the crowd like Blacks at a Ku Klux Klan convention.

Detectives Jackson and Viccers, because of Mrs. Payne's statement, came to the funeral to both escort her and observe the crowd. You know, detect the murderers. Those who might have wanted Mr. Payne dead. It seems as if almost everyone at this funeral (or celebration, as it appeared), with the exception of Mr. Payne's family, were glad he was gone. There was a mood of jubilation. Yes, the

festival or carnival came to town. It seemed as if many of
these people wanted to make sure Mr. Payne was definitely,
positively, securely and assuredly dead. He was. Quite.

The services were held at Christ Jesus Apostolic Rapture
Preparation Cathedral, the Pentecostal church Mrs. Payne
was a member of. "Would you get a load of that name,"
Detective Jackson said to Viccers. As he changed his voice to
his version of a typical southern Baptist minister he said, as
if he were a radio announcer, "Greetings from the St. Paul
Macedonia Evolutionary, Back to Africa by way of the U-S
of A Revolutionary Missionary Baptist Cha-uch!" "So, they
should just call it 'Church'?" Viccers asked. "All I'm sayin' is
what happened to Cathedral Apostolic Church?"

The choir sang exhilarating, foot-stomping songs as the
congregation stood up, clapped and swayed to the jumping
beats, which penetrated the floor and the pews. It was difficult to remain still while the choir sang.

The minister began his message. Throughout the message,
the members screamed amen, waved their hands as if they
were slapping someone and clapped their hands signifying
their apparent approval of the minister's sermon. Now, when
he really said something that "tickled their fancy," they'd jump
up and point in his direction, "You betta preach past-ta,"
they'd say. He titled his message, "Strangers Be Ware" and his
topic came from a scripture in the Bible which, paraphrased
says, "Depart from me you workers of iniquity, I know you
not." The minister told the people that they should e prepared
before they die—that they would not make it to heaven if they

were a stranger to God. As the minister lifted his left leg, cuffed his right hand to his right ear, held the mic in his left hand and tremulously shook his head and body he screamed, "YOU must kno-oo-oow Him! You see, you gotta know Him for yourself! Don't be a stranger to God? Oh, don't be deceived, my friend, you can go to church all you want. You can sing in the choir all you want, you can usher people down the church isles every Sunday, and you can play that organ until your finger tips sting, but don't let the devil fool you, honey. Knowing Him means a lot more than that. It's a way of life. It's talking to Him in the morning. Talking to Him in the evening. Talking to Him late in the midnight hour. It's talking to Him while you're driving you car. Talking to Him while you're running your four miles.

"Now, let's not get technical. We all know He is omniscient and omnipresent. He knows everything. Yes, all there is to know about you! He knew you before you knew yourself. Now, I just met this funeral director today. But do I know Him? If someone asks me tomorrow if I know Him, I might say yes. But, do I really know him? Let me make it plain for you."

"Make it plain past-ta," someone replied from the congregation.

"You see, the Lord requires an intimate relationship with us. A CLOSE relationship. They he spelled out the word "CLOSE" and said, "That is, *C*—Commune with Him daily. *L*—Love Him unconditionally. *O*—Obey His commandments. *S*—Surrender ALL to Him and be Saved like the Bible says? And you'll live with Him *E*—Eternally! If you don't have a C-L-O-S-E relationship with God, you're a stranger to Him, sugar. And if you're a stranger to Him you better be ware!"

At that point the church blasted into a thunderous explosion of exaltation and Detective Jackson leaned over to his partner and said, "Boy, he kinda makes you want to go to church every Sunday, huh?" Viccers chided back, "You just need to go to church!"

Almost everyone went to the gravesite, including Paula Daley. Unlike the first day the detectives met her, she looked quite feminine at the funeral. She was donned in a form-fitting dress and her hair was in a french roll instead of the ponytail she sported when they saw her in the office. She smiled at the detectives and attempted to comfort Katie, who surprisingly didn't shed a tear during the service. As the funeral attendees greeted the family after the committal of the body to the ground, Mrs. Payne introduced some of the detectives, particularly the women who were involved in the session she mentioned in her statement.

First to shake Mrs. Payne's hands and to be introduced to the detectives was Jazmyn Hemphill, Mr. Payne's recently hired law clerk. Ms. Hemphill wore a form fitting lycra spandex black dress which unashamedly exhibited her non-deprived and adequate bosom. She wore sunglasses, and didn't smile at all; although her face looked pleasantly pleased. "Good afternoon," she said to the detectives as she sashayed to her car. The detectives tried to get a look at Ms.

Hemphill's boyfriend but they couldn't see him from where they were.

Next, Mrs. Payne introduced the detectives to Lynette Carroll and her daughter, Tyffani, who cried on and off throughout the service. Tyffani, although she was Mr. Payne's daughter, was not allowed to be with the family because only a few people knew Mr. Payne was her father. Ms. Carroll, who was of average height, with a heavily creamed coffee complexion, wore a black suit, a turquoise blouse and a black hat, accented with a turquoise ribbon. "Lynette," Mrs. Payne said as she looked in the detectives direction, "this is Detective Jackson and Detective Viccers." "Detectives," Ms. Carroll said as she snatched her hand away and shook her head. "Girl, they don't suspect that you had anything to do with this, do they?" "Mrs. Carroll," Viccers interjected. "Rest assured, we are merely trying to solve this case. Everything is routine, we assure you. Routine." "Humph" she moaned as she grabbed her daughter's arm and stormed away.

"I'm so sorry, Katie," was the next voice they heard. It was the voice of Rosalind Gayland, they were told with a brief introduction. "I know," was Mrs. Payne's response. "No, Katie, I'm sorry about everything," Ms. Gayland said as she leaned her slender and tall frame down to hug Mrs. Payne. "Everything, Katie. You have to be the most upstanding woman I know. You don't deserve any of this. Call me if you need anything. And I mean anything! Gentlemen," Ms. Gayland said as she looked in the Detectives direction, "take care of Katie. She's a gem. Take care of her," she repeated as she walked away with her head hanging.

Finally, they were introduced to Theresa Johnson. As she removed her shades to reveal her large hazel eyes, her modestly sized nose and her adequate lips, she nodded as she greeted the detectives. "Katie," she said in a firm yet soft voice, "I want you to be happy. I'm not going to pretend that this unfortunate incident hasn't in some way eased my temporary pain. However, I should only think about you now. No matter what you may believe, Katie," Mrs. Johnson continued, "I never wanted to hurt you. Never. I hope you can forgive me." "Forgiven," Mrs. Payne said humbly as Ms. Johnson kissed her on the cheek then walked away.

After stepping away from Mrs. Payne, Detective Jackson motioned to Viccers to step away from Mrs. Payne also, then he whispered to his partner, "Get a load of this Mrs. Payne. Can you believe anyone could be so nice? She must've done it. She's too much of a saint to be innocent. She's guilty. Or crazy—one. How you just gonna allow some floozy, who was supposed to be your friend, who you just found out had been sleepin' with your husband, just come up in your face and say all that. And then kiss you on the cheek. She gives turning the other cheek a new name. No! Something's wrong with this picture. If that were my Maggie, she would have slapped the slut from her to Africa and snatched her back again. 'Forgiven,'" he said as he sarcastically mimicked Mrs. Payne. "Who does she think she's fooling?"

"Look, Dale," Detective Viccers said to his partner. "There are some good people in the world and Mrs. Payne seems to be one of them."

"Yeah, but she sure is letting these, I don't know what to call 'em, sluts, get away with murder."

"I don't know if I'd call them sluts. None of these women look squalid."

"Man, there you go with those words again. Now what the heck does *squalid* mean?" Jackson asked. Viccers began to define the word for him. Detective Jackson cut him off in mid-sentence and said, "Man, do you think you're really all that? I have a pretty extensive vocabulary, I just don't feel you have to fake and share. Be real. Talk real.

"That's what's wrong with us today. Ebonics." Viccers shook his head, then he sarcastically repeated Jackson's last words. "Be real. Talk real. I guess what you're really telling me is, Be stupid—Talk stupid."

"You calling me stupid?"

"No, but I am calling your way of thinking stupid."

"Who does it harm?"

"Your children and other children. Our children mimic us. If we allow them to talk that way they'll become accustomed to it and it will just be that much more difficult for us to fix their speech later."

"Whatever, man! My kids are excellent students. Now, getting back to the discussion at hand, I think Mrs. Payne seems to be satisfied with the way things worked out. She doesn't seem innocent."

"I believe she's innocent."

"Well, Detective Dale Jackson replied, "I believed she was innocent too; until I witnessed that little charade back there. No one can be that nice. No one. Man, her neck should be tired from turning her cheek so much." Jackson laughed and shook his head and continued, "It's as if her husband was a stranger to her. She didn't know him. and, on top of that, she's pleasant with all of these women too. Just-a-smilin'— like 'Oh, well, it's not their fault.' What's wrong with her?"

"Yeah," Viccers added, "but, apparently he was a stranger to all those women too. None of them knew he had been messing around with the world. None except the psychologist. And she says she stopped spending time with him over twenty years ago—Right?"

"That's right," Jackson agreed as they walked toward Mrs. Payne to escort her to the car. From that distance the two detectives saw that Mrs. Payne was talking to her children. They decided to continue talking for a while to give her a chance to converse with her son and daughter. The children appeared to be normal and happy young people. The oldest, Candace Payne, is 16 and the youngest, Leyton, is 15. They were both dressed to suit children whose parents made above average incomes. Both teenagers were still wiping the tears from their eyes. Candace's eyes were swollen and her face was puffy as she hugged her mother and didn't seem to want to let go. Mrs. Payne's mother, Victoria Perkins, walked to her daughter's side and attempted to console her.

The detectives allowed Katie Payne to talk with her mother and children for a while, then they took her back to the county facility. As they drove off Mrs. Payne waved at her children and her mother, blew a kiss to them, allowed her chin to meet her chest and remained with her head hung in that position until they reached their destination.

Twelve

"I know who killed Emory Payne. Meet me at the Boulevard Cafe, near Magic's Theatre on King Boulevard. I only want to talk to you, not the short fat guy. He seems a bit uptight. I'll wear red," Detective Viccers stood speechless as he read this note, which was left crumpled on his chair at the station and signed 'Anonymous'. "Hey, Dale," Viccers said as he threw the crinkled note to his partner, "look at this." Jackson studied the note and then said with a perplexed expression on his face, "Not the fat guy? I'm not fat!" Simultaneously, Dale Jackson adjusted his pants by pulling them over his adequately sized round tummy and exclaimed, "Why'd he want you? I'm in charge of this case. Not you! Something is strange about this."

"You know Dale," Viccers shook his right index finger in the air as if he just received the answer to a problematic question and said, "you're not the solution to every problem. You just don't know why someone would think I was more capable of detecting a criminal than you, huh. You narcissistic fool, you!"

"Wrong!"

"Right! You're a self-centered, egocentric man with a Napoleon complex."

"Oh, so now you're callin' me names. So much for being a Christian."

"I'm calling it as it is. Anyway, you have any idea which one of the ladies wrote this note?" Viccers asked.

"You see. That's what I mean. You're not ready!"

"What do you mean?"

"Who says this is woman who wrote this note."

"There are only women involved in this case. He seemed to only have female enemies."

"Eliminate no one until proof eliminates them! You're just not ready to venture on your own yet. You're not seasoned!"

"I'm not? Well, guess what, I'm on my way to the Boulevard Care—Not you!"

Viccers walked out of the station, head held arrogantly high, and with his back facing Jackson waved his hand good-bye and said, "See ya!" Those last words of Viccers' rang in Jackson's ears as he followed Viccers to the Café.

***

Detective Randall Viccers graduated with a Bachelors degree in Political Science from Howard University in Washington, D.C. and a Master's degree in Criminology from George Washington University. He is extremely finicky and expects everything to be in order according to his standards. After sharing an office for five months with Jackson, their Caption was forced with the decision of whether he should allow Jackson to have his own office after Viccers complained about the "pig sty" that he and Jackson shared. Viccers submitted a letter to Captain Capria stating:

> *"I can no longer work productively in the pig-sty of an office of which I share with Detective Dale Jackson. Although he is both a brilliant and established detective, who I am fortunate to have been afforded the opportunity to he the apprentice and work with, I will be forced to resign my position with this department if my working environment is not changed immediately. I propose a change of offices only, not the partner pairing. Detective Jackson is an exceptional detective whom I have benefited from immensely. It is my opinion that Detective Jackson is the most accomplished and conversant detective in this department. The valuable lessons I have learned while working with Detective Jackson are immeasurable. However, Detective Jackson is also the most disorganized human being I have ever met and I absolutely abhor sharing an office with him. Additionally, this change would prove advantageous to the department as the many important pieces of evidence that can potentially be lost in the array of client*

documents scattered around his office, in what I must say is the most unsystematic filing system I've ever witnessed. I will keep these items in my office. In, of course, an orderly fashion."

"So, Jackson, Captain Capria said after Detective Jackson read the letter which his partner wrote, "What do you have to say for yourself?"

"Look Cap," Jackson responded. "Some people are unnecessarily picky. But usually they are women. Viccers has had this shoe in his behind since I met him. We are detectives not princesses or fairies!"

"I like a clean office. Are you calling me a fairy?"

"No sir Cap. It's his mentality. His approach. His actions. Just like a woman."

"Look, Jackson—your office condition is going to have to change!"

"Yes sir."

"He's right! You need to have a better system. That office must be cleaned over the weekend and it must be kept clean. Understood?"

"Sure."

"Now you know Viccers came with the highest recommendations. We expect him to follow in your footsteps and continue to uncover the varied crimes in this area. This office is ridiculous. I don't bother you because I know you do your job well and you find anything you need in here. But, we couldn't leave an elephant in here for fear he'd get lost."

"C'mon Cap, that's a low blow. We'd see his trunk."

"This isn't funny Jackson.

"Okay Cap. But, in 27 years on the force I've always solved my cases. That means I ain't ever lost no evidence. None. So, neither you nor that 'kiss-up', too good, bourgeoisie brotha' have a valid reason why I should change a system that has worked all these years."

"You may think Randall Viccers doesn't have a valid reason to want a clean office, but I do. Unless there are changes made over the weekend I'll take you off the MacArthur case!"

"You can't do that Cap! I'm too close to solving that case!"

"Wanna try me?" With that last comment, the Captain slammed the door as he left.

"Take me off the MacArthur case," Jackson thought as the Captain left.

The MacArthur case was, at first, a highly publicized lawsuit involving the Securities Exchange Commission in which three agents were being sued. The plaintiffs cited numerous claims for relief including, fraud (for intentional misrepresentations and negligence), breach of fiduciary duty, professional negligence, and RICO. A. Donald MacArthur, who was the first name plaintiff of this class action lawsuit, would have most likely been the victor in this matter. He, as outlined in his complaint, along with the entire class, sought both compensatory, punitive and exemplary damages totaling a staggering $50 million. Surprisingly, or not so surprisingly, A. Donald MacArthur was murdered shortly after he was deposed by opposing counsel. In less than two weeks, three other plaintiffs involved in the lawsuit were also murdered. It was an extremely hot case and Jackson did not want to let it go. He cleaned his office without further objection.

Jackson never became the tidy man Viccers wanted him to be, but he became more conscious of where he put evidence and other important documents.

***

Viccers drove to King Boulevard, where he was to meet this anonymous person at the café. Jackson had followed him, but he parked behind the old swap meet located on the corner of the block. Through his binoculars he could see Viccers enter the restaurant. Shortly after Viccers went in, Jackson saw a man, dressed in red, donned in sunglasses and a hat, go in the restaurant (fitting the description in Viccers' note).

Viccers sat at a table in the corner of the restaurant near a window with a view of King Bouelvard. He was staring out of the window as the anonymous person, unbeknownst to Viccers, sat in the seat across from him.

"It's me," the stranger said as he kicked Viccers' feet under the table.

"Hi," Viccers replied. "I understand you have some evidence that might be helpful to the Payne murder and that you specifically requested that I come instead of my partner. But I must inform you that I am not the lead detective on this case. I am…" and before Viccers could finish his introduction, the nameless man interjected.

"First, let me tell you that I will do all the talking here. I am not going to answer any questions and I am not going to release any additional information other that what I offer.

"I know you're an intelligent man," the anonymous man whispered in a deep throaty voice. "You graduated top in your class at Howard U. You initially wanted to be an attorney, but the excitement and fulfillment of being a detective pleased you more. Actually, the truth of the matter is you didn't pass the New York bar exam after two tries, so you did what you had to make a living. Yes, Detective Viccers, I know you graduated from law school. You did extremely well as a matter of fact. It was just that darn bar exam," the stranger said as he laughed sinisterly. Viccers sat accros from this mysterious man with a perplexed and amazed look on his face. As Viccers started to open his mouth to speak, his table partner cleared his throat then raised his index finger past his mouth and then slowly scratched the tip of his nose. Viccers caught his hint and did not utter a word.

"Emory Payne was a snake. A venomous animal, who should have died the way he did. So don't be deceived, I offer this killer not for his sake but for the sake of an innocent person, who I will not name.

"I've written the killer's name on a piece of Mr. Payne's stationery which is inside this envelope. There's also some receipts which verify the purchases of the many items bought to accomplish the bombing. Too many lives have been hurt by Emory Payne and my friend needs help." On his last word, he stood up. Viccers grabbed his arm and asked, "Could you tell me what this person's motive was for killing Mr. Payne?" "I told you detective, no questions," the man said as he left the restaurant just as he came in, quickly.

Viccers walked out of the restaurant. He contemplated whether he should open the envelope or wait until he arrived at the station. Viccers stopped suddenly because he heard someone hissing at him. As he looked around near the side of a building heard a voice say, "Over here, stupid." Over here." Viccers walked around to the side of the building and to his surprise he saw his partner, Jackson. Jackson looked at the envelope in his partner's hand and said, "You haven't opened that yet!"

"What are you doing here Jackson?"

"Taking care of your sorry behind."

"I don't need your assistance. I'm doing just fine alone. So, what did your being here do to assist me?"

"Did you get his name?"

"No. So, am I to believe you did?"

"Did you see what kind of car he was in?

"No!"

"Did you get his license plate number?"

"Well, if I didn't see his car, wouldn't it be safe to assume that I didn't get his license plate."

"Well, I got his license plate number. And that's why you need my assistance."

"California plates?"

"Yeah."

"New car, old car?"

"Old."

Viccers started walking toward his car. Jackson followed behind him. Viccers was angry. He thought Jackson did not trust him enough to take care of this situation on his own. He decided not to tell him any information. As Viccers opened his car door, Jackson sat on the passenger side. Jackson knew that Viccers was attempting to bother him by not immediately telling him what happened inside. So, in an effort to beat Viccers at his own game, Jackson took the copy of the Ebony Magazine from under his arm, cleared his throat and pretended to peruse an article. "Man, that Sheryl Lee Ralph is a looker, isn't she. You know, she stars in that show with that teenage singer my kids like. Ah, what's her name?" Jackson paused as he tilted his head back and scratched his chin, Tequilla or something. No, that's not it. But she's named after a drink."

"BRANDY," Viccers announced abruptly.

"Yes, that's it. Brandy. That's her name. Did you catch those awards the other night?" He never took a breath because he didn't want Viccers to interrupt him just yet—he was on a roll. "Man, but no one has come out with a dress like Toni Braxton's that other year. Man, I love women."

"You always have to win, don't you?" Viccers asked as he shook his head.

"What's bothering you Vic?" Jackson smiled, happy that he accomplished the task he set out to.

"You know what I'm talking about."

"Well I'm asking you to tell me."

"Do you want to know what happened in there or not?"

"That's right. You went in there to get some information. Didn't you? So, what ya' get?"

"He gave me this envelope. He said that he wrote the killer's name on a piece of Emory Payne's stationery."

"Did you ask him why we should trust him?"

"No. He told me he wouldn't answer any of my questions."

"Well, what are you waiting for? Open it!"

Viccers opened the envelope and he shook his head. As he handed his partner the envelope he said, "You won't believe who did it."

"You mean who he said did it," Jackson said as he snatched the paper from Viccers. "Humph," Jackson sighed. "We better bring all those women in for questioning."

Thirteen

Jackson walked into his home at about ten o'clock in the evening. His wife, Maggie, as he affectionately called her, was in the kitchen preparing a snack for him.

"Hi honey," Margaret said to Jackson.

"Baby, you didn't have to stay up because of me."

"Well, after you called to tell me you were on your way, I thought you might need a little something in your stomach before you went to bed. Plus, from the sound of your voice, I thought you might need someone to talk to."

"I don't deserve you Maggie. It's been a rough day though. You know, I've been through so many murder cases, but this one bothers me a little bit more than the others."

"Why?"

"All these women were involved with this one man. A few knew it, most didn't."

"Some men get all the luck, huh?"

"No. I wouldn't want that headache."

"What bothers you about it? I mean, besides the obvious moral issues."

"I guess because they were all friends. They all shared a common past. You know? I've heard of men cheating. But he was trifling. I wouldn't even honor him by calling him a dog."

"Yeah. But, some of those women were trifling too. They shouldn't have been involved with their so-called friend's boyfriend, fiancé or husband. Whatever he was to her when they were involved with him. It already hurts when a person finds out that their significant other has been having an affair. But, to find out that it's been with one of your good friends is a nightmare. I'm sure that would drive any person to entertain thoughts of hurting someone. Then, she has to find out that all of her friends have been with her husband. I couldn't handle it!"

"So you think she did it?"

"Dale, I just sympathize with how she must have been feeling. Of course I don't condone violence of any sort. But I do understand pain."

"But, do you think she did it?"

"Look, I don't know if you've told me everything about the case. But, if you did, no. From what I understand, she just doesn't seem to be capable of such a cruel crime. Evidently, she believed her husband had been loyal to her. I think whoever committed this crime has had a lot of time to think about it and had been angry for a long time. You know, you never told me who's name was in the envelope."

"We began questioning the ladies today."

"So that means you're not going to tell me."

"We're going to question the young lady, Jazmyn Hemphill, tomorrow."

"So you're not saying."

"Maggie, you know I don't get terribly specific with my cases. It's bad luck. I'll tell you when it's solved."

"I'll know by then. So, do you all suspect this Jazmyn…what was her last name?"

"Hemphill. Baby, everyone is a suspect right now. Everyone. You know that."

"Think she did it?"

"I'll be able to answer that question better tomorrow."

"Oh, you're that close to a solution?"

"We'll talk more tomorrow. Now, let's get some other action going on. I need a little stress relief. And, you know there's nothing like some good ole fashion lovin' from my baby to relieve my tensions."

"You are sick, tired and old. Come on, let's go to bed."

"Now that's what I'm talking about!"

***

Jazmyn Hemphil entered the precinct. She sat perfectly straight and seemingly confident. Donned in her signature sunglasses, her head was held high and her face firm, as she put her coach bag in her lap. Stoic. No smile. No emotion. Just there.

"Ms. Jackson," a short clerk announced as she peered over her cat framed glasses at Jazmyn, "the detectives will see you now. It's the first office to your left."

"Thank you," Jazmyn replied as she walked confidently. Just as she took her first step, her boyfriend, Darcel Redding, ran and grabbed her arm.

"Darcel," she was surprised to see him.

"Who else?"

"Why are you here?"

"To support you."

"I don't need any support. I'll be okay. I don't want you to get involved in this."

"Well, I'm here just in case you do."

"I'll be okay, Darcel."

"I know you will Jazz, I know you will."

"What if I don't want you to go in with me?"

"Then, I might have to make you angry with me. I'm going in Jazmyn."

"The detectives might not let you."

"We'll see. If not, I'll be right out here for you."

"Come right in Ms. Hemphill," Detective Viccers said as he turned to Darcel and asked, "Who are you? You look familiar."

"I'm Darcel Redding, Jazmyn's boyfriend and I'd like to come in with her."

"I'm sorry, no one else is allowed in during the questioning."

Ms. Hemphill sat at the table across from both Detectives Jackson and Viccers.

"Ms. Hemphill, state your name," Detective Jackson said.

"Jazmyn Rosalind Hemphill."

"I am Detective Dale Jackson and this is my partner, Detective Randall Viccers. I will be primarily conducting the questioning today. First, Ms. Hemphill, tell us where you were born."

"Bakersfield, California."

"How did you come to live here in Los Angeles? Did your family move here?"

"No. I just came to find my roots."

"To find your roots?"

"Yes. To find out more about my family."

"Your parents couldn't tell you?"

"Aren't these questions personal."

"We'll ask the questions. Now, parents couldn't tell you?

"No."

"Why not?'

"I thought the purpose of this questioning was regarding the investigation of the murder of Emory Payne. Not my personal life."

"You're right, Ms. Hemphill. But, in our investigation we cannot discount any information. Personal or otherwise. So, if you don't tell us, we will find out."

"I an tell you that without your invading my personal files. I was employed by Mr. Payne as his legal assistant."

"We know that Ms. Hemphill. But, what we don't know is why a young man dressed in disguise, would give us your name as Mr. Payne's killer."

"What! I have no idea either. Why would you believe this man? Who is he?"

"Again, Ms. Hemphill, we'll ask the questions. Why would you murder Mr. Emory Payne?"

"I wouldn't and I didn't!"

"We have reason to believe that you did."

"Well, I didn't! What evidence do you have. It must be purely hearsay because I didn't kill him. Some man off the street tells you all something and you believe him. It's not true. I couldn't murder that man, even if I wanted to!"

"Why? Is it because he's your father?"

"What's makes you think that?"

"The informant. Medical records. Adoption records. Little things like that."

"Okay. So, why would I kill my father?"

"Because he didn't want you. Because he had other children that he took care of. You were the oldest and you didn't understand why he couldn't provide for you too. You were angry. Angry enough to kill!"

"Okay! I've been angry for years. But, not angry enough to kill someone. I'm not insane!"

"Maybe you were temporarily."

"I didn't kill him!"

"Why did you start working for Mr. Payne?"

"I wanted to see if he could lead me to my natural mother."

"How would he do that?"

"I don't know. I thought she might come around to see him from time to time. I really didn't want him to know who I was. I didn't even want to get to know him. I just wanted to meet her. My father, my adoptive father, spoke so highly of her."

"How did you find out about your natural father?"

"My adoptive father, who raised me, told me about my birth father and my birth mother. I've known I was adopted ever since I can remember. He told me that my mother was intelligent and kind. He said she was a remarkable woman and he knew her personally. He told me that she cared for me, but my father convinced her that she would do me more harm than good.

"Anyway, as a high school graduation gift to me, my father gave me a treasure chest that my mother prepared for me when I was born. There was a handwritten note from her apologizing for bringing me into this world the wrong way. Basically, she said that this was her way of helping me and making what was wrong right.

"I asked my father how did he get this information. I knew my mother must have been very close to him. I didn't know why my mother trusted me with him. He told me that my mother believed I was being adopted to a middle class family in Bakersfield. My father went along with my mother to meet the couple and sign the papers.

"What my mother didn't know is that my adoptive father had already made arrangements with this couple that he would take me immediately and they were to never discuss these arrangements with my mother or any other authority.

"I've never met my adoptive father's family. I didn't think he had family while I was growing up. It was just the two of us. He was the best father anyone could have. But I could tell he was bitter. He didn't like my natural father. He would mention him from time to time. But, he never mentioned his name. All my life, whenever he mentioned my mother, he wore a huge smile. I always thought they must have had a thing going on. You know, for him to remain so fond with her, to take on her child and not have any contact with her.

"Well, in my birth mother's letter she mentioned that she and her Uncle George took care of me for three months. After reading that sentence, I dropped the letter. I began to cry. My father held me and said he was so sorry he didn't tell me."

"Why did you begin to cry Ms. Hemphill?" Detective Viccers asked, as Detective Jackson rolled his eyes and said, "And you're the one with all the degrees!"

"Well, my father's name is George Hemphill and he is my natural mother's uncle. He raised me by himself and he never married. He stopped speaking to my mother, his niece, after she gave me up for adoption. He knew she would be angry that he kept me.

"My father, I mean my Uncle, showed me pictures of my natural father and mother. But they were old pictures. Nothing recent. He told me where my father worked and where my mother worked. He kept up with their lives. I found out that he knew a lot about both of them. He was the brother of my mother's mother. He never introduced me to her either. No one in the family. And, he made me promise never to tell my mother if I found her. I grew even more fond of my father, because I knew he must have loved my mother, dearly.

"Anyway, my father was somewhat upset when I told him that I wanted to meet my natural father and mother. But, he understood my curiosity. I was only eighteen and I didn't know what to do. I did not bother to see either of my birth parents at the time. I knew my natural father was an attorney and that was the career I wanted to chose. So, after my second year in law school, I applied for a summer internship with him, Emory Payne. He turned me down. However, he called me a few months ago and that's when I started working for him.

"My father told me that I resembled my mother. So, I was reluctant to meet her. So, I never tried. After meeting my biological father's wife and family, I thought he was happy and I didn't want to interfere. But, I still wanted to see my mother—even from a distance."

"Ms. Hemphill," Detective Jackson interrupted. "We were told that you were one of the individuals who attended a session at Ms. Gayland's office. Is that correct?"

"Yes."

"Tell us about that."

"That was an eventful day."

"Okay. Go on."

"One day this lady came in to meet with Mr. Payne's bookkeeper, Paula Daley. I saw her waiting and asked if she needed any help. She said her name was Rosalind Gayland

and that she came to have lunch with Ms. Daley. I almost lost my cool because I knew she was my mother. I knew her name. I saw the resemblance. She told me that I looked familiar and then asked me if I would like to be a part of one of her sessions. I began stuttering. She asked me if I was okay. Then, I spilled my coffee on an original transcript of one of our important clients. I told her I would be honored to participate in one of her sessions.

"My father told me that my biological father was a dog. But, I didn't know how much. After each of those women discussed what he had done to them, I became nauseated. If it weren't for my natural mother and that poor Mrs. Payne, I would have told them who I was too. Instead, I became angry. Enraged. So, I left the session. Without one word! But I didn't kill him! I wouldn't waste my time.

"I stormed into Mr. Payne's office and I told him who I was. I told him who raised me. I told him about the confessions at Ms. Gayland's, my biological mother's, office. He was nonchalant. Crude even. He threatened to tell her and to bring legal actions against my father regarding my adoption. I told him I hoped something terrible would happen to him. I told him that his actions caused insurmountable pain in a lot of lives. He just sat there. Callous and uncaring.

"I ran out of his office and called my father. I told him everything! Everything. He told me to come home immediately. I told him that I would just stay with Darcel because I didn't feel like driving. This was the same day that Mr. Payne was murdered. But, I didn't murder him."

"Where is your father?—I mean Mr. George Hemphill."

"He's ahh," she paused as she looked down and then up again. "At home. I hope he's okay. When I called him and told him that I was being brought in for questioning, he became very upset. He almost started hyperventilating. I asked him was he okay. He told me that he would be okay and that he needed to tell me something and that I should sit down. I told him that I was walking out the door and that I would call him as soon as I came back home. He just said, "Call me, please call me. Better yet, come home when you're finished." I told him I would call him first and then I'd decide when I was coming home. I asked him was he okay again. He told me that he loved me very much and that he would be okay."

"Do you think he did it?"

"No! My father has a heart of gold. He raised me when he didn't have to. He loved me. He took care of me. He was intelligent and kind. He couldn't have done anything like this."

"What is his address?"

Ms. Hemphill gave the detectives the address. They called the police department in Bakersfield and a car was sent out to the Hemphill home.

***

When the Bakersfield police arrived at the Hemphill address, they noticed that the door was open. Mr. Hemphill was at a desk in a makeshift office in the house. He was slumped over the desk with a pen in his hand. The note he began writing read:

> *My dear Jazmyn:*
>
> *I am beginning to have severe chest pains. So, I don't know if I can wait for you. I love you. I loved your mother. I loved my sister. Your mother was hurt, I wanted to help her and I didn't want her to lose you. Emory needed to die. He needed to pay. I made sure that he did. He can't hurt you or your mother ever again. It had to be done. He couldn't threaten your mother and then threaten you too. I couldn't allow it. I hope I didn't disappoint you. I did it because I love you. I'm sor...*

Mr. Hemphill died before he finished the note.

Fourteen

Rosalind Gayland stood at the precinct with flowers in her hand for her friend, Katie Payne. Rosalind kept in contact with Katie every day. They talked much and cried often. Katie asked Rosalind to pick her up from the prison when she was informed that she was to be released. Katie informed the detectives that Rosalind was going to pick her up. Before she left, the detectives requested that they speak with both her and Rosalind Gayland.

When Katie walked in the room, after being released, she and Rosalind began crying and hugged each other. Rosalind apologized to her friend for the secrets for all these years. She reiterated to Katie that all of this would not have happened had she known Katie from the beginning. Katie still wasn't sure of what happened, entirely. The detectives told them that they found the killer of Emory Payne and who he was. "After all of the new found mysteries, the killer is a male," was Katie Payne's comment. "Yes, Mrs. Payne, your husband's killer was a man," Detective Dale Jackson replied.

"Was a man?"

"Yes."

"You mean someone else has died."

"Yes."

"Did he kill himself?"

"No ma'am."

The detectives, of course, proceeded to inform Katie Payne of all the particulars in connection with her husband's tragic and untimely demise. Mrs. Payne was astonished to discover that Jazmyn was actually her husband, Emory's, daughter. "His daughter!" she exclaimed. "You're telling me that there was yet another woman involved in this multi lover's triangle?" "Yes," Detective Jackson stated.

Mrs. Payne asked, "Well, who is the killer? And who is Jazmyn's mother?

"By way of a note we found near his body, Mr. George Hemphill of Bakersfield, California confessed to the killing of Mr. Payne. He was found dead in his home. Apparently, he hated Mr. Payne for what he did to his great niece, Jazmyn, or I should say, Roselyn Hemphill, and his niece, Rosalind Gayland."

Rosalind began to cry. "You mean my Uncle George is dead. And, he raised Roselyn, I mean Jazmyn. Do you mean Jazmyn is my baby? He kept her all these years without telling me?"

"Yes, Ms. Gayland," Detective Jackson said. "We found a separate note for you at Mr. Hemphill's home. We made a copy for you. We need to retain the original letter as evidence."

"Jazmyn," Rosalind cried. "Where's Jazmyn? So, she knew who I was all along?" As Rosalind uttered those words,

Jazmyn Hemphill stood at the doorway. They walked slowly toward each other and both began to cry—for their Uncle George, who expressed his love for them, and for each other. Then, they embraced and rocked in each other's arms. "You're so beautiful Jazmyn," Rosalind said to her daughter she never knew. "I'm glad I finally met you. I wish my father, I mean our Uncle George, could have witnessed our meeting. He spoke so highly of you. He loved you so much. He said you were his favorite niece," Jazmyn said to the mother she never knew.

"I'm sorry that Emory caused so much pain in each of your lives," Katie Payne said to her friend Rosalind and her daughter, Jazmyn. Both Rosalind and Jazmyn hugged Mrs. Katie Payne, and they cried together. "I guess I really didn't know the man I was so madly in love with and was married to for so many years. He was merely a stranger that I knew. A Known Stranger."

***

Detectives Dale Jackson and Randall Viccers watched Mrs. Payne, Rosalind Gayland and Jazmyn Hemphill leave the station. It was a dark, dreary and wet California day. They each were relieved the case was solved. "You know," Detective Jackson chided. "I still wonder whether that fourth ticket was for Mrs. Payne's mother." "Of course it was," Detective Viccers stated, "she has proven herself to be an honest and faithful woman."

"I wish all of our cases could end on some happy note."

"I don't think it was such a happy note. Mrs. Payne discovered she really didn't know her husband, she now has to deal with his death and, she'll have to tell her two children about their father. If she doesn't, the newspapers will. Then Rosalind Gayland and Jazmyn Hemphill have to go bury their uncle this week. All because of Emory Payne."

"Is that Cap calling us?"

"Yeah, that's him."

"Here he comes."

"Jackson and Viccers I need you to go over to Parker High School right away," Cap demanded. "There's been a murder. You can complete your paper work on the Payne case later this week. You've released the Payne woman, right?" "Yeah. What happened at Parker High?" Jackson asked. "Parker's Vice Principal found the Principal's body in the girls locker room this morning," Cap said. "She said she saw a female student leave the scene. Get over there!" Captain Capria turned around and went back into the station.

"Now we can't even go home and get some rest," Jackson said as he looked at Viccers. "Yeah," Viccers agreed, "Let's go take care of this. I'd like to see my wife some time soon."

"Me too," Jackson stated. "Come on, I'll drive."

"I'm not getting back in your filthy and funky car."

"And I'm not driving with your slow behind."

"Well, I'll drive a little faster because I refuse to get in your vehicle."

"*I refuse to get in your vehicle.* Why don't you shut up! Sissy."

"Will you stop calling me those names."

"You're right, I shouldn't call you *those* names. Okay, I'll stop calling you *those* names when you stop acting like a sissy."

"Well, I don't care what you call me, as long as I'm driving."

"Just drive man, drive!" "Sissy," Jackson said under his breath where Viccers could not hear him.

"Off to Parker High School," Viccers said, "This one should be a piece of cake."

Jackson's reply, "We'll see…"

Epilogue

The Known Stranger is a part of a four book series regarding the murder cases assigned to Detectives Dale Jackson and Randall Viccers. Jackson and Viccers are two opposite personalities who often experience conflict, but work well together in finding solutions to Los Angeles' many murder mysteries. In each of their cases, you will discover an innovative twist that will keep you spellbound.

Look for the second book in this series, *Principal Deceit*, to be released soon. The once exemplary reputation of an upstanding and well known Los Angeles principal is questioned after he is found dead in the girls locker room of Parker High School. Varied rumors regarding the murder run rampant throughout the school and the city. One individual, other than the principal, knows who the killer is. Everyone's talking, but no one's listening. (*This is your first clue.*) Join Detectives Jackson and Viccers as they unveil the answer to this mystery. Is it elementary?

About the Author

Rachelle H. Guillory attended California State University, Dominguez Hills. Prior to this work, Ms. Guillory self-published *Expressions of Soul*, a collection of her original poetry. Soon to be released is her second novel *Lord I Want A Man...Can I Get An Amen?* a novel chronicling the lives of six female friends and their seemingly endless pursuit to find a good man. Ms. Guillory resides in Inglewood, California with her two children, Jazmyn Childress and Dale Childress II. Look for the upcoming release of the second book in this series, *Principal Deceit.*

9 780595 094592